Bob Dylan expressing the inexpressible
So,
what *is* Tarantula about?
It's about a lawyer who leads his pig around on a leash and takes his paranoia seriously. (The lawyer's or the pig's? Or the author's?)
It's about a police chief who's had his name engraved on his personal bazooka.
About Jesus Christ as just another meathead.
About Truman Peyote (*that* rings a bell), and Tom who ought to have been called Bill.
And other curious things.
It's finally about Bob Dylan thinking aloud.
So? What's special about Bob Dylan thinking aloud?
This – from the introduction by his American publishers: 'Poets and writers tell us how *we* feel by telling us how *they* feel.'
Go along with that fundamental statement – as the present publishers do – and *Tarantula*'s a book for you.

Born in 1941, Bob Dylan is widely revered as America's greatest living popular songwriter. In the course of a career that has spanned over forty years, he has acted as voice-piece and chronicler to several generations, and was one of the first to channel public feeling about racial discrimination and the Vietnam war into popular protest songs. Combining an acute awareness of the zeitgeist with absurdist humour, Dylan struck a chord with millions. In 2004, Bob Dylan published the first volume of his autobiography, *Chronicles*.

Also by Bob Dylan

Chronicles: Volume One
Lyrics: 1962–2001

TARANTULA

BOB DYLAN

HARPER PERENNIAL

London, New York, Toronto and Sydney

Harper Perennial
An imprint of HarperCollins*Publishers*
77–85 Fulham Palace Road
Hammersmith
London W6 8JB

www.harperperennial.co.uk

This edition published by Harper Perennial 2005
6

Previously published in paperback by Panther 1973

First published in Great Britain by MacGibbon & Kee Ltd 1971

A catalogue record for this book
is available from the British Library

This novel is entirely a work of fiction. The names, characters
and incidents portrayed in it are the work of the author's
imagination. Any resemblance to actual persons, living
or dead, events or localities is entirely coincidental.

ISBN 978 0 00 721504 1

Typeset in Stempel Garamond by Palimpsest Book Production Limited,
Polmont, Stirlingshire
Printed and bound in Great Britain by Clays Ltd, St Ives plc

TARANTULA

Guns, the Falcon's Mouthbook & Gashcat Unpunished

aretha/ crystal jukebox queen of hymn & him diffused in drunk transfusion wound would heed sweet soundwave crippled & cry salute to oh great particular el dorado reel & ye battered personal god but she cannot she the leader of whom when ye follow, she cannot she has no back she cannot . . . beneath black flowery railroad fans & fig leaf shades & dogs of all nite joes, grow like arches & cures the harmonica battalions of bitter cowards, bones & bygones while what steadier louder the moans & arms of funeral landlord with one passionate kiss rehearse from dusk & climbing into the bushes with some favorite enemy ripping the postage stamps & crazy mailmen & waving all rank & familiar ambition than that itself, is needed to know that mother is not a lady . . . aretha with no goals, eternally single & one step soft of heaven/ let it be understood that she owns this melody along with her emotional diplomats & her earth & her musical secrets

    the censor in a twelve wheel drive semi
    stopping in for donuts & pinching the
    waitress/ he likes his women raw & with
    syrup/ he has his mind set on becoming
    a famous soldier

manuscript nitemare of cut throat high & low & behold the prophesying blind allegiance to law fox, monthly cupid & the intoxicating ghosts of dogma . . . nay & may the boatmen in bathrobes be banished forever & anointed into the shelves of alive hell, the unimaginative sleep, repetition without change & fat sheriffs who watch for doom in the mattress . . . hallaluyah & bossman of the hobos cometh & ordaining the spiritual gypsy davy camp now being infiltrated by foreign dictator, the pink FBI & the interrogating unknown failures of peacetime as holy & silver & blessed with the texture of kaleidoscope & the sandal girl . . . to dream of dancing pillhead virgins & wandering apollo at the pipe organ/ unscientific ramblers & the pretty things lucky & lifting their lips & handing down looks & regards from the shoulders of adam & eve's minstrel peekaboo . . . passing on the chance to bludgeon the tough spirits & the deed holders into fishlike buffoons & yanking ye erratic purpose . . . surrendering to persuasion, the crime against people, that be ranked alongside murder & while doctors, teachers, bankers & sewer cleaners fight for their rights, they must now be horribly generous . . . & into the march now where tab hunter leads with his thunderbird/ pearl bailey stomps him against a buick & where poverty, a perfection of neptune's unused clients, plays hide & seek & escaping into the who goes there? & now's not the time to act silly, so wear your big boots & jump on the garbage clowns, the hourly rate & the enema men & where junior senators & goblins rip off tops of question marks & their wives make pies & go now & throw some pies in the face & ride the blinds & into aretha's religious thighs & movement find ye your nymph of no conscience & bombing out your young sensitive dignity just to see once & for all if there are holes & music in the universe & watch her tame

the sea horse/ aretha, pegged by choir boys & other pearls
of mamas as too gloomy a much of witchy & dont you
know no happy songs

　　the lawyer leading a pig on a leash
　　stopping in for tea & eating the censor's
　　donut by mistake/ he likes to lie about
　　his age & takes his paranoia seriously

the hospitable grave being advertised & given away in
whims & journals the housewife sits on. finding herself
financed, ruptured but never censored in & also never
flushing herself/ she denies her corpse the courage to crawl-
close his own door, the ability to die of bank robbery &
now catches the heels of old stars making scary movies on
her dirt & her face & not everybody can dig her now. she
is private property . . . bazookas in the nest & weapons of
ice & of weatherproof flinch & they twitter, make scars &
kill babies among lady shame good looks & her constant
foe, tom sawyer of the breakfast cereal causing all females
paying no attention to this toilet massacre to be hereafter
called LONZO & must walk the streets of life forever with
lazy people having nothing to do but fight over women
. . . everybody knows by now that wars are caused by
money & greed & charity organizations/ the housewife is
not here. she is running for congress

　　the senator dressed like an austrian
　　sheep. stopping in for coffee & insulting
　　the lawyer/ he is on a prune diet &

secretly wishes he was bing crosby
but would settle for being a close
relative of edgar bergen

passing the sugar to iron man of the bottles who arrives
with the grin & a heatlamp & he's pushing 'who dunnit'
buttons this year & he is a love monger at first sight . . .
you have seen him sprout up from a dumb hill bully into
a bunch of backslap & he's wise & he speaks to everyone
as if they just answered the door/ he dont like people that
say he comes from the monkeys but nevertheless he is dull
& he is destroyingly boring . . . while Allah the cook scrapes
hunger from his floor & pounding it into the floating dishes
with roaring & the rest of the meatheads praising each
other's power & argue over acne & recite calendars &
pointing to each other's garments & liquid & disperse into
segments & die crazy deaths & bellowing farce mortal farm
vomit & why for Jesus Christ be Just another meathead?
when all the tontos & heyboy lose their legs trying to frug
while kemosabe & mr palladin spend their off hours
remaining separate but equal & anyway why not wait for
laughter to straighten the works out meantime & WOWEE
smash & the rage of it all when former lover cowboy
hanging upside down & Suzy Q. the angel putting new
dime into this adoption machine as out squirts a symbol
squawking & freezing & crashing into the bowels of some
hideous soap box & it's a rumble & iron man picking up
his 'who dunnit' buttons & giving them away free & trying
to make friends & even tho youre belonging to no polit-
ical party, youre now prepared, prepared to remember
something about something

the chief of police holding a bazooka
with his name engraved on it. coming in
drunk & putting the barrel into the face
of the lawyer's pig. once a wife beater,
he became a professional boxer & received
a club foot/ he would literally like to
become an executioner. what he doesnt know
is that the lawyer's pig has made friends
with the senator

gambler's passion & his slave, the sparrow & he's ranting
from a box of black platform & mesmerizing this ball of
daredevils to stay in the morning & dont bust from the
factories/ everyone expecting to be born with whom they
love & theyre not & theyve been let down, theyve been
lied to & now the organizers must bring the oxen in &
dragging leaflets & gangrene enthusiasm, ratfinks & suicide
tanks from the pay phones to the housing developments
& it usually starts to rain for a while . . . little boys cannot
go out & play & new men in bulldozers come in every
hour delivering groceries & care packages being sent from
las vegas . . . & nephews of the coffee bean expert & other
favorite sons graduating with a pompadour & cum laude-
praise be & a wailing farewell to releasing the hermit &
beautifully ugly & fingering eternity come down & save
your lambs & butchers & strike the roses with its rightful
patsy odor . . . & grampa scarecrow's got the tiny little
wren & see for yourself while saving him too/ look down
oh great Romantic. you who can predict from every posi-
tion, you who know that everybody's not a Job or a Nero
nor a J.C. Penney . . . look down & seize your gambler's
passion, make high wire experts into heroes, presidents into

con men. turn the eventual . . . but the hermits being not talking & lower class or insane or in prison . . . & they dont work in the factories anyway

> the good samaritan coming in with the
> words 'round & round we go' tattooed on
> his cheek/ he tells the senator to stop
> insulting the lawyer/ he would like to
> be an entertainer & brags that he is
> one of the best strangers around, the
> pig jumps on him & starts eating his
> face

illiterate coins of two head wrestling with window washer who's been reincarnated from a garden hoe & after once being pushed around happily & casually hitting a rock once in a while is now bitter hung up on finding some inferior. he bites into the window ledge & by singing 'what'll we do with the baby-o' to thirsty peasant girls wanting a drink from his pail, he is thinking he is some kind of success but he's getting his kicks telling one of the two headed coins that tom jefferson used to use him around the house when the bad stuff was growing . . . the lawrence welk people inside the window, theyre running the city planning division & they hibernate & feeding their summers by conversing with poor people's shadows & other ambulance drivers, & they dont even notice this window washer while the families who tell of the boogey men & theyre precious & there's pictures of them playing golf & getting blacker & they wear oil in the window washer's union hall & these people consider themselves gourmets for not attending charlie starkweather's funeral ye gads the champagne being appropriate pagan & the buffalo, tho the restaurant owners are vague about it, is fast disappearing into violence/ soon there will be but one side of the coin & mohammed wherever he comes from, cursing & window washers falling & then no one will have any money . . . broad save the clean, the minorities & liberace's countryside.

> the truck driver coming in with a carpet
> sweeper under his eyes/ everybody says
> 'hi joe' & he says 'joe the fellow that
> owns this place. i'm just a scientist. i
> aint got no name' the truck driver hates
> anybody that carries a tennis racket/ he
> drinks all the senator's coffee & proceeds
> to put him in a headlock

first you snap your hair down & try to tie up the kicking voices on a table & then the sales department people with names like Gus & Peg & Judy the Wrench & Nadine with worms in her fruit & Bernice Bearface blowing her brains on Butch & theyre all enthused over locker rooms & vegetables & Muggs he goes to sleep on your neck talking shop & divorces & headline causes & if you cant say get off my neck, you just answer him & wink & wait for some morbid reply & the liberty bell ringing when you dont dare ask yourself how do you feel for God's sake & what's one more face? & the difference between a lifetime of goons & holes, company pigs & beggars & cancer critics learning yoga with raving petty gangsters in one act plays with V-eight engines all being tossed in the river & combined in a stolen mirror . . . compared to the big day when you discover lord byron shotting craps in the morgue with his pants off & he's eating a picture of jean paul belmondo & he offers you a piece of green lightbulb & you realize that nobody's told you about This & that life is not so simple after all . . . in fact that it's no more than something to read & light cigarettes with . . . Lem the Clam tho, he really gives a damn if dale really does get nailed slamming down the scotch & then going outside with Maurice, who aint the Peoria Kid & dont look the same as they do in Des Moines, Iowa & good old debbie, she comes along & both her & dale, they start shacking up in the newspapers & jesus who can blame 'em? & Amen & oh lordy, & how the parades dont need your money baby . . . it's the confetti & one george washington & Nadine who comes running & says where's Gus? & she's salty about the bread he's been making off her worms while dollars becoming pieces of paper . . . but people kill for paper & anyway you cant buy a thrill with a dollar as long as pricetags, the end of the means & only as big as your fist & they dangle from a pot of golden rainbow . . . which attacks & which covers the saddles of noseless poets & wonder blazing & some- where over the rainbow & blinding my married lover into the ovation maniacs/ cremating innocent child into scrapheap for vicious controversy & screwball & who's to tell charlie to stop & not come back for garbage men arent serious & they gonna get murdered tomorrow & next march 7th by the same kids & their fathers & their uncles & all the rest of these people that would make leadbelly a pet . . . they will always kill garbage men & wiping the smells but this rainbow, she goes off behind a pillar & some- times a tornado destroys the drugstores & floods bring polio & leaving Gus & Peg twisted in the volleyball net &

Butch hiding in madison square garden . . . Bearface dead from a flying piece of grass! I.Q. – somewhere in the sixties & twentieth century & so sing aretha . . . sing mainstream into orbit! sing the cowbells home! sing misty . . . sing for the barber & when youre found guilty of not owning a cavalry & not helping the dancer with laryngitis . . . misleading valentino's pirates to the indians or perhaps not lending a hand to the deaf pacifist in his sailor jail . . . it then must be time for you to rest & learn new songs . . . forgiving nothing for you have done nothing & make love to the noble scrubwoman

what a drag it gets to be. writing
for this chosen few. writing for
anyone cpt you. you, daisy mae, who are
not even of the masses . . . funny thing,
tho, is that youre not even dead yet . . .
i will nail my words to this paper,
an fly them on to you. an forget about
them . . . thank you for the time.
youre kind.
        love an kisses
        your double
        Silly Eyes (in airplane trouble)

Having a Weird Drink with the long Tall Stranger

back betty, black bready blam de lam! bloody had a baby blam de lam! hire the handicapped blam de lam! put him on the wheel blam de lam! burn him in the coffee blam de lam! cut him with a fish knife blam de lam! send him off to college & pet him with a drumstick blam de lam! boil him in the cookbook blam de lam! fix him up an elephant blam de lam! sell him to the doctors blam de lam . . . back betty, big bready blam de lam! betty had a milkman, blam de lam! sent him to the chain gang blam de lam! fixed him up a navel, blam de lam (hold that tit while i git it. Hold it right there while i hit it . . . blam!) fed him lotza girdles, raised him in pneumonia . . . black bloody, itty bitty, blam de lam! said he had a lampchop, blam de lam! had him in a stocking, stuck artichokes in his ears, planted him in green beans & stuck him on a compass blam de lam! last time i seed him, blam de lam! he was standing in a window, blam de lam! hundred floors up, blam de lam! with his prayers & his pig-foot, blam de lam! black betty, black betty blam de lam! betty had a loser blam de lam, i spied him on the ocean with a long string of muslims – blam de lam! all going quack quack . . . blam de lam! all going quack quack. blam!

    sorry to say, but i'm going
    to have to return your ring.
    it's nothing personal, excpt

that i cant do a thing with
my finger & it's already
beginning to smell like an
eyeball! you know, like i like
to look weird, but nevertheless,
when i play my banjo on stage, i
have to wear a glove. needless
to say, it has started to affect
my playing. please believe me.
it has nothing whatsoever to
do with my love for you . . .
in fact, sending the ring back
should make my love for you
grow all the more profound . . .

> say hi to your doctor
> love,
> Toby Celery

(Pointless Like a Witch)

trip into the light here abraham . . . what about this boss
of yours? & dont tell me that you just do what youre told!
i might not be hip to your sign language but i come in
peace. i seek knowledge. in exchange for some informa-
tion, i will give you my fats domino records, some his an

hers towels & your own private press secretary . . . come
on. fall down here. my mind is blank. i've no hostility. my
eyes are two used car lots. i will offer you a cup of urn
cleaner – we can learn from each other/ just dont try &
touch my kid

got too drunk last nite. musta drunk
too much. woke up this morning with
my mind on freedom & my head feeling
like the inside of a prune . . . am
planning to lecture today on police
brutality. come if you can get away.
see you when you arrive. write me
when youre coming

your friend,
homer the slut

Ballad in Plain Be Flat

the feet were stuck between the petticoat & tom dick &
harry rode by & they all screamed . . . her lips was so small
& she had trenchmouth & when i saw what i had done, i
guard my face/ the time is handled by some crazy cheer-
leader snob & sticking her tongue out, dropping a purple

tostle cap, she mingles with a bus, caresses a bloody crucifix & is praying for her purse to be stolen up gun-powder alley! her name, Delia, she envies the block of chain & kingdom where the khaki thermometer kid, obviously a front man & getting a commission growling 'she'll drown you! split your eyes! put your mind where your mouth is! see it explode! just 65 & she dont mind dying!' is bending over for scraps of food, fighting an epileptic fit & trying to keep dry in a typical cincinnati weather . . . Claudette, the sandman's pupil, wounded in her fifth year in the business & she's only 15 & go ahead ask her what she thinks of married men & governors & shriner conventions go ahead ask her & Delia, who's called Debra when she walks around in her nurse uniform, she casts off pure light in the cellar & has principles/ ask her for a paper favor & she gives you a geranium poem . . . chicago? the hogbutcher! meat-packer! whatever! who cares? it's also like cleveland! like cincinnati! i gave my love a cherry. sure you did. did she tell you how it tasted? what? you also gave her a chicken? fool! no wonder you want to start a revolution

look. i dont care what your daddy
says. j. edgar hoover is just not that
good a guy. like he must have
information on every person inside the
white house that if the public knew
about, could destroy those people/
if any of the knowledge that he's
got ever got out, are you kidding,
the whole country would probably
quit their jobs & revolt. he aint never
gonna lose his job. he will resign with

honor. you just wait & see . . . cant you figure
out all this commie business for yourself?
you know, like how long can car thieves
terrify the nation? gotta go. there's a
fire engine chasing me. see you when i get
my degree. i'm going crazy without you.
cant see enough movies

> your crippled lover,
> benjamin turtle

On Busting the Sound Barrier

the neon dobro's F hole twang & climax from disap-
pointing lyrics of upstreet outlaw mattress while pawing
visiting trophies & prop up drifter with the bag on head
in bed with next of kin to the naked shade – a tattletale
heart & wolf of silver drizzle inevitable threatening a
womb with the opening of rusty puddle, bottomless,
a rude awakening & gone frozen with dreams of birthday
fog/ in a boxspring of sadly without candle sitting &
depending on a blemished guide, you do not feel so gross
important/ success, her nostrils whimper. the elder fables
& slain kings & inhale manners of furious proportion,
exhale them against a glassy mud . . . to dread misery of
watery bandwagons, grotesque & vomiting into the

flowers of additional help to future treason & telling horrid
stories of yesterday's influence/ may these voices join with
agony & the bells & melt their thousand sonnets now . . .
while the moth ball woman, white, so sweet, shrinks on
her radiator, far away & watches in with her telescope/
you will sit sick with coldness & in an unenchanted closet
. . . being relieved only by your dark jamaican friend –
you will draw a mouth on the lightbulb so it can laugh
more freely

 forget about where youre bound.
 youre bound for a three octave
 fantastic hexagram. you'll see
 it. dont worry. you are Not bound
 to pick wildwood flowers . . . like
 i said, youre bound for a three
 octave titanic tantagram
    your little squirrel,
    Pety, the Wheatstraw

Thermometer Dropping

the original undertaker, Jane, with bangs, & her hysteri-
cal bodyguard, Coo, who comes from Jersey & always
carries his lunch/ they screech around the corner & tie

the old buick into a lamppost/ along came three bach-
elors sprinkling the sidewalk with fish/ they spot the mess.
first bachelor, Constantine, he winks at second bachelor,
Luther, who immediately takes off his shoes & hangs them
around his neck. George Custer IV, third bachelor, weary
from trying to chew up a stork, takes out his harmonica
& hands it to first bachelor, Constantine, who after
twisting it into form of a fork, reaches into shoulder
holster of the bodyguard, removes a sickle, & replaces it
with this out of shape musical instrument . . . Luther
begins to whistle 'Comin thru the Rye' George IV gives
out with a wee chuckle . . . all three continue down the
avenue & dump the leftover fish into the unemployment
office. all except of course for a few trout, which they
give to the lady at the lost & found/ accident is reported
at 3 P.M. it is ten below zero

do people tell you to your
face youve changed? do you
feel offended? are you seeking
companionship? are you plump?
4ft. 5? if you fit & are
a full blooded alcoholic
catholic, please call
UH2-6969
　　　　　ask for Oompa

Prelude to the Flatpick

mama/ tho i make no attempt to disqualify the somber
moody you. mama with the woeful shepherd on your
shoulder. the twenty cent diamond on your finger. i play
no more with my soul like a tinker toy/ i now have the
eyes of a camel & sleep on a hook . . . to glorify your trials
would be most easy but you are not the queen – the sound
is queen/ you are the princess . . . & i have been your
honeyed ground. you have been my guest & i shall not
smite you

> 'are there any questions?' the
> instructor asks. a blond haired
> little boy in the first row
> raises his hands an asks
> 'how far to mexico?'

poor optical muse known as uncle & carrying a chunk of
wind & trees from the meadow & the kind of uncle that
says 'holy moly' in a mild whisper meeting the farmer who
say 'here. have some hunger for you.' & lay some good
fine work in his nauseous lap/ chamber of commerce tries
to tell poor muse that minnesota fats was from Kansas &
not so fat, just notoriously heavy but they're putting up
supermarket across the meadow & that should take care of
the farmer

                    'does anybody wanna be anything
                    out of the ordinary?' asks the
                    instructor, the smartest kid
                    in class, who comes to school
                    drunk, raises his hand & says
                    'yes, sir. i'd like to be a
                    dollar sir'

the dada weatherman comes out of the library after being
beaten up by a bunch of hoods inside/ he opens up the
mailbox, climbs in & goes to sleep/ the hoods come out /
tho they dont know it, theyve been infiltrated by a bunch
of religious fanatics . . . the whole group looks around for
some easy prey . . . & settle for some out of work movie
usher, who is wearing a blanket & a pilot's cap/ it is one
second to fourth of july & he does not fight back/ the dada
weatherman gets mailed to Monaco, grace kelly has another
kid & all the hoods turn into drunken business men

                    'who can tell me the name of
                    the third president of the
                    united states?' a girl with
                    her back full of ink raises
                    her hand & says 'ernest tubb'

more blue pills father & gobble the little quaint pills/ these
gushing swans, rituals & chickens in your sleep – theyve
been given the ok & the mad search warrant yes & you,
the famous Viking, snatching the time bomb from Sophia's
filter tip, down some jack daniels & get out there to meet

James Cagney . . . a swinging armadillo for your friend, your faithful mob & mona lisa behind you . . . God ma, the swains are baking him & how i wish i could ease him & honor him with peace thru his veins, make him calm. almighty & slay the horrible hippopotamus of his nitemare . . . but i can take no martyr's name nor sleep myself in any gust of dungeon & am sick with cavity . . . ludicrous, the dead angel, monopolizing my vocal cords, gathering her parent sheep onward & homeward into obituary. she's hostile. she's ancient . . . aretha-golden sweet/ whose naked-ness is a piercing thing – she's like a vine/ your lucky tongue shall not decay me

    'is there anyone in class who
    can tell me the exact hour his
    or her father isnt home?' asks
    the instructor. everybody
    suddenly drops their pencils
    & runs out the door – all excpt
    of course the boy in the last
    row wearing glasses & who's
    carrying an apple

juicy roses to coughing hands assembling & pluck national anthems! all hail! the football field ablaze with doves & alleyways where hitchhikers wandering & setting fire to their pockets resounding with the nuns & tramps & discarding the weedy Syrian, surfs of half-reason, the jack & jills & wax Michael from the church acre, who cry in their prime & gag of their twins . . . empty ships on the desert & traffic cops on the broomstick &

weeping & hanging onto a goofy sledgehammer & all the
trombones coming apart, the xylophones cracking & flute
players losing their intimates . . . as the whole band
groaning throwing away measures & heartbeats while it
pays to know who your friends are but it also pays to
know you aint got any friends . . . like it pays to know
what your friends aint got – it's friendlier to got what
you pay for

down with you sam, down with your
answers too. hitler did not change
history. hitler WAS history/ sure
you can teach people to be beautiful,
but dont you know that there's a
greater force than you that teaches
them to be gullible – yeah it's called
the problem force/ they assign
everybody problems/ your problem is that you
wanna better word for world . . .
you cannot kill what lives an expct
nobody to take notice. history is alive/
it breathes/ now cut out that jive/
go count your fish. gotta go. someone's
coming to tame my shrew. hope they
removed your lung successfully. say hi
to your sister

love,
Wimp, Your
Friendly Pirate

Maria on a Floating Barge

in a sunburned land winter sleeps with a snowy head at the west of the bed/Madonna. Mary of the Temple. Jane Russell. Angelina the Whore. all these women, their tears could make oceans/ in a deserted refrigerator carton, little boys on ash wednesday make ready for war & for genius . . . whereas the weary archaic gypsy – yawning – warbles a belch & tracking the cats – withstanding a ratsized cockroach she hardly appears & looks down upon her sensual arena

> dear fang, how goes it old buddy?
> long time. no see. guess what? was
> gonna vote for goldwater cause you
> know, he was the underdog but then
> i found out about this jenkins thing,
> & i figger it ain't much, but it's
> the only thing he does have going
> for him so i'm changing my vote to
> johnson. did you get the clothes i
> sent you? the shirt used to belong
> to sammy snead so better take good care
> of it
>
>   see you
>   Mouse

Sand in the Mouth of the Movie Star

a strange man we're calling Simply That wakes up to find 'what' scribbled in his garden, he washes himself with a scrambled egg, puts his glasses in his pants & pulls up his trousers, there's a census taker knocking on his door & his orders for the day are nailed up on his mailbox reading that the route on junky monday is therefore as follows: two pints of soft liberty. a book of zulu sayings. citizen kane translated into dirty french. an orange t.v. studio. three bibles each autographed by the hillbilly singer who can sing salty dog the fastest. the back page of a 1941 daily worker. a salty dog. any daughter of any district judge. a tablespoon of coke & sugar heated to 300 degrees. jack london's left ear. seven pieces of deadly passport. a corn on the cob. five wooden pillows. one boy scout resembling charlie chan & a stolen titerope walker/ 'what' is in my garden, he says over the phone to his friend, wally the fireman/ wally replies 'i dont know. i really couldnt say. i'm not there' the man says 'what do you mean, you dont know! what is written in my garden' wally says 'what?' the man says 'that's right' . . . wally replies that he is on his way down a pole & asks the man if he sees any relationship between doris day & tarzan? the man says 'no, but i have some james baldwin & hemingway books' 'not good enough' says wally, who again asks 'what about a shrimp & an american flag? do you see any relationship between those two things?' the man says, 'no, but i see bergman movies & i like stravinsky quite a lot' wally tries again & says 'could you tell me in a million words what

the bill of rights has to do with a feather?' the man thinks
for a minute & says 'no i cant do that but i'm a great fan
of henry miller' wally slams the phone & the man, Simply
That, he gets back into bed & begins reading 'The Meaning
of an Orange' in german . . . but by nitefall, he is bored.
puts the book down & goes to shave while looking into
a picture of thomas edison/ he decided over a bowl of milk
to go out & have a good time & he opens the door &
who's standing there but the census taker 'i'm just a friend
of the person who lives here' he says & goes back into the
house & out the back door & down the street & into a
bar with a moose head . . . the bartender gives him a double
brandy, punches him in the groin & pushes him into a
phone booth – obviously the man's crime is that he sees
nothing resembling anything – he wipes the blood away
from his groin with a hankie & decides to wait for a call/
'what' is still written in his garden, the clinics are inte-
grated. the sun is still yellow. some people would say it's
chicken . . . wally's going down a pole, the census taker
arrives to make a phone call & phone booths dont have
back doors/ junky monday driving, going down a one way
street & turning into a friday the 13th . . . Ah wilderness!
darkness! & Simply That

        went five hours without a drink
        of water. figger i'm ready for
        the desert. wanna come? i'll
        take along my dog. he's always
        good for a laugh, pick yuh up
        at seven

                                    faithfully,
                                    Pig

23

Roping Off the Madman's Corner

green maggie of profanity slapstick & her cast of seven
coats shining & fighting the milkmaids & high whining
barndoor slam – heavens! & righteous 38–20 slightly built
on the ball & chain & leashing the lawyer's pigeon while
the rock n roll lead guitar player does his mother's violets
& his thing in the middle of the bailiff's workbench &
green maggie pushing you into hotrod driver's eyes & he's
lisping & he has no money to pay for his language &
maggie's not green & not funny & life gets unbearable but
the orator is not the reporter & hanging around at the
press room & shelling out to the day crew & merchants
of venice & why be bothered with other people's set ups?
it only leads to torture/ why it's incredible! the world is
mad with justice

> dear mayor wagner. has anybody
> ever told you, you look like
> james arness? i am writing to
> say that you are my son's idol.
> could you please send your
> schedule & repertoire to him, with
> an autographed picture, at your
> earliest convenience. he would
> appreciate it kindly as that's
> all he does is play your records
> & defend you to his friends.

i do hope it's you that's reading
this & not some secretary
                    thank you
                    wishfully
                    Willy Purple

Saying Hello to Unpublished Maria

you taste like candy TUS HUESOS VIBRAN yowee &
i'm here because i'm starving & swallowing your tricks
into my stomach ERES COMO MAGIA like the greasy
hotel owner & it's not your father i'm hungry for! but i
will bring a box for him to play with. i am not a cannibal!
dig yourself! i am not a sky diver/ i carry no sticks of
dynamite . . . you say NO SERE TU NOVIA & i am not
a pilgrim neither TU CAMPESINA & you dont see ME
crying over that i cant be sad & wonderful & yippee TU
FORMA EXTRANA your horseness amazes me/ i will
stand – oh honorable – on the window of your countess
even tho i am not a window shade & bang SOLO SOY
UN GUITARRISTA all i do is drink & eat. all i have is
yours

i'm telling you, the next time you
threaten to commit suicide in front
of me, i'm just gonna haul off an blow
your brains out y'hear! y'read me?
i'm so sick of having you bring me
down that i'd just as soon tie you
up & ship you off to red china.
another thing! you better take
good care of my mother. if i
hear that youre taking out your
misery on her, i'm coming to see
what i can do about things once &
for all . . . why dont you learn to
dance instead of looking for new
friends? dont you know that all
the friends have been taken

                              yours,
                              Hector Schmector

Forty Links of Chain (A Poem)

fox eyes from abilene – garbage poet from the
greyhound circuit & who has a feeling for the most
    lost
pieces of frost & boast of glass jaw & grampa

playing tiddlywinks & finks in the sinks & the
   barf &
gook in the book
of his cook, the ma & he's back in town
screwing around
with his hairlip down . . . he needs a dime &
writing rhyme You
dont have to guess . . . you know
the rest/ watch his nose! you can see where he goes
by offering to pay his dues – fox eyes, he's
got lotza blues – Tiny the chick with the wet
   newspaper,
she used to bring french fries to the mechanics &
whose right arm once went deaf & dumb
(it can happen to some)
she sees fox eyes come
climbing out of the stop sign & he's got a hangover
on top of it & she say 'oh great grooby fox eyes,
   lead me to the
garbage' & he take her by the
lilywhitecottonpickin
hand & she say 'yeah man i be a yellow monkey
   oowee!'
& he say 'jus you folly me baby snooks! jus you folly
me & you feel fine!' & she say 'giddy up & hi ho
   silver &
i feel irish!' & both go off & get a bus schedule & she
saying all the time 'steady big fella! steady!' while on
the other side of the street this mailman who looks
   like
shirley temple & who's carrying a lollypop stops &
looks at a cloud & just then the sky, he gets kinda
   pissed

& decides to throw his weight around a little &
 bloop a
tulip falls dead – the mailman starts talking to a
 parking
meter & fox eyes, he say 'it sure wasn't like this in
abilene' & it's a hurricane & a bus reading baltimore
leaves them in a total mess – she falls on her knees &
she say 'i'm filthy' & fox eyes he say 'go back to
florida baby there ain't nothing here a city grill like
you can do' & the chick she does a handstand & she
 say
'i'm canadian!' & he say 'get outa here & go to
 florida!'
& she starts reciting fox eyes poems about salvation
 & the
loony bin, strikes in the coloring book factory &
 christmas
when they wrapped him in a shirt & he say
 'WHOA! GET OUTA
HERE! I STEAL YO MONEY OWEE JESUS
 GRILL! YOU SOME SLUMP!'
& she moans & groans & she say 'oh i really do
 love life &
love love & love living & he say 'grooby! wail!
 wail!' &
she say 'dont you understand' & she starts making
 this terrible
scene right there in the middle of the street . . .
Tiny- -i met Tiny
later at an outrageous party – she was sitting under
 a clock & i say
'you need an umbrella, friend' & she say, 'oh no!
 not another one!'

& she's got a new boyfriend now & he looks like
   machine gun kelly . . .
fox eyes – he lost all his money in a furnace – when
   last heard from
was riding fast freight out of salinas in a pile of
   lettuce &
still trying to collect unemployment . . . me? i made
   a special trip
downtown to get some graveyard figures – but it
   wasnt raining &
there were no buses going to baltimore/ just a
   broken jawed parking meter,
a water logged pen & a bunch of old shirley temple
   pictures
with her neck in a noose was all that i could find
look. i dont care if you are
a merchant marine. the next time
you start telling me i dont
walk right, i'm gonna get some
surfer to slap your face. i think
youre being very paranoid about
the whole thing . . . see you at the
wedding
                         stompingly yours
                         Lazy Henry

Mouthful of Loving Choke

crow jane from the wedding into the beast nest where wild man peter the greek & ambassador frenchy do primitive worship with hustling john from coney striking a pose & dancing the pink velvet – all dramatics & curiously belonging to the armenian hunchback resembling arthur murray who's very turned off & gets syphilis & crow jane, she gets the chilly blues watching but she speaks like a champion & she dont kid around 'what you gonna do? i mean besides now's time for the good men promenade a party?' some plaintive woos in the twilight & throats ripping & laughing & fool's terror snapping like a tail & taking it in the ribs & bop music where south walls quivering & colliding bosoms & weigh the likes of maid marian's bandits & i repeat: two face minny, the army derelict/ christine, who's hung up on your forehead/ steve canyon jones who looks like mae west in a closet/ screwy herman x, who looks like a closet/ jake the brown, who looks like a forehead . . . dino, the limping bartender, who steps in between Man Mountain Sinatra who looks like the boy next door & Gorging George, who has no last name . . . all these and their agents & 'how come you so smart crow jane?' & she say back 'how come you wanna talk so colored? & dont call me no crow jane!' & super-freak pushing & shoving amazing – totally amazing – '& i think i'm gonna do april or so is a cruel month & how you like your blue eyed boy NOW mr octopus?' when the four star colonels come in & everybody says yankee doodle & plastered & some western union boy rides thru

on a unicycle yelling 'God save the secrets!' but is just
coming on – he's mad & he's a horseshoe wizard – nobody
cares tho & he's looking for the action & nobody cares
about that either & he yells 'help!' & two face minny,
screaming, swinging from a chandelier & goes to bless him
'you cant make nobody understand you too smart to think
you know anything! not even john henry did that' crow
jane jingle girl & she's a phantom & mouth like an oven
& she dances on a cake of islam & 'dont tell someone what
you know they already know. that makes them think that
you just like them & you aint!' . . . but then you take
gwendeline, the different story & rides with lawrence of
arabia & plays with her mercury – mumbling crummy
world & 'oh, the sadness!' . . . she gets some horny
foreigners' attention but mainly all the cool people
continue drawing noses on robert frost books 'why be
crazy on purpose?' say two face minny who's now on top
the western union boy & steve canyon jones going off in
the corner & crying 'we aint never gonna get no messages
that way!' . . . crow jane, she got this talent for robbing
hardware stores & always being someplace at the wrong
time but saying the right things 'dont do your ideas –
everybody's got those – let the ideas do you & talk with
melody & money tempts ideas & it cant get close to melody
& take all the money you can get but dont hurt nobody'
crow jane, she got class '& above all else, be all else!' oh
the nites with broken arcs, the backs of greensleeves &
bruised film – homely & absurd with rhythm & it gets to
you after a while . . . a glass sidewalk meeting the cracker
boy's soul & trees like fire hydrants standing in the path of
the wooden horse & help mama! help those that cannot
understand not to understand . . . the cracker boy wears
spiked shoes but his hands are bare/ peter & frenchy still

dancing the cocktail tango – the hunchback being carried
out . . . honeymoon locked into footsteps of the riderless
stallion/ rome falling with driving wishy washy half note
– crawl with the blues feeling . . . & the going daylight.
crow jane say come, hang out her limelight . . . there are
green bullets in my throat/ i walk sloplily on the sun feeling
them turn into yellow keys – i touch jane on the inside &
i swallow

        dear tom
        have i ever told you that i
        think your name ought to be
        bill. it doesnt really matter
        of course, but you know, i like
        to be comfortable around people.
        how is margy? or martha? or
        whatever the hell her name is?
        listen: when you arrive & you
        hear somebody yelling 'willy' it'll
        be me that's who . . . so c'mon. there'll
        be a car & a party waiting. it'll
        be very easy to single me out, so
        dont say you didnt know i was there

                                gratefully
                                truman peyote

The Horse Race

'. . . always trying, always gaining'
                                    – lyndon johnson

yes & so anyway on the seventh day, He created pogo, bat
masterson, & a rose colored diving board for His cronies/
the sky already strung up shivered like the top of a tent.
'what's all this commotion' he said to his main man,
Gonzalas, who without batting an eyelash picked up a rake
& began flogging a cloud . . . seeing that Gonzalas had the
wrong idea, He told him to lay down the rake & go to
build an ark/ when Gonzalas reaches twenty-five he starts
wondering when his parents will kick off. it's nothing
personal, it's just that he needs some money & is begin-
ning to resent the fact that he hasnt been laid yet/ 'why
did you not create an eighth day?' ask Gonzalas' chauffeur
to his Sausage Maker on the steps of the boom boom parlor/
while handing in his perfume/ the sky, changing into a sexy
spaghetti odor, continues to tremble – Gonzalas, mean-
while sports a cane & tries to hide his korean accent/ edgar
allan poe steps out from behind a burning bush . . . He
sees edgar. He looks down & says 'it's not your time yet'
& strikes him dead . . . Gonzalas enters/ places fifth in the
second

   how come youre so afraid of
   things that dont make any

33

sense to you? do people pass
you up on the street all the
time? do cars pass you up on
the highway? how come youre
so afraid of things that dont
make any sense to you? do you
water your raisins daily? do
you have any raisins? is there
anything that does make sense
to you? are you afraid of twelve
button suits? how come youre
so afraid to stop talking?

your valve cleaner
Tubba

Pocketful of Scoundrel

in a hilarious grave of fruit hides the wee gunfighter – a
warm bottle of roominghouse juice in the rim of his sheep-
skin/ lord thomas of the nightingales, bird of youth,
rasputin the clod, galileo the regular guy & max, the novice
chess player/ the battles inside their souls & gloves being
as dead as their legends but only more work for the living
jesters – victims of assassination & dying comes easy . . .
on the other side of the tombstone, the amateur villain

sleeps with his tongue out & his head inside the pillow case/ nothing makes him seem different/ he goes unnoticed anyway.

> dear Sabu
> it's my chick! she tells me that
> she takes long walks in the woods.
> the funny thing about it is that
> i followed her one nite, & she's
> telling me the truth. i try to
> get her interested in things
> like guns an football, but all
> she does is close her eyes &
> say 'i dont believe this is happening'
> last nite she tried to hang herself . . .
> i immediately thought of having her
> committed, but goddam she's my chick.
> & everybody'd just look at me funny
> for living with a crazy woman.
> perhaps if i bought her her own car,
> it would help/ can you fix it?
> thanx for listening
All Petered Out

Mr. Useless Says Good-bye to Labor & Cuts a Record

Phombus Pucker, with his big fat grin. his hole in the head. his matter of fact knowledge of zen firecrackers. his little white lies. his visions of sugar plums. his dishwater hands/ Phombus Tucker. with his bulldog wit. his theories on atomic nipples. his beard & his backache/ Bombus Thucker. with his soft boiled stovepipe. his aloneness & aloofness. his hatred for crap/ Longus Bucker. with his numbers & decimals. with his own special originality . . . spent hours & hours carving his name in the sand. when all of a sudden, a wave's commotion washed him & his name right into the ocean (ho ho ho)

        look, you know i dont wanna
        come on ungrateful, but that
        warren report, you know as well
        as me, just didn't make it. you know.
        like they might as well have
        asked some banana salesman from
        des moines, who was up in toronto
        on the big day, if he saw anyone
        around looking suspicious/ or better
        yet, they just coulda come & asked me
        what i saw/ the doctors say i gotta tumor
        coming up tho, so i got more important things
        to do than to be bothered with straightening

out this whole mess . . . while youre down
there, see if you can get me murph the
surf's autograph

bye for now
your lightingman
Sledge

Advice to Tiger's Brother

you are in the rainstorm now where your cousins seek
raw glory near the bridge & the lumberjacks tell you of
exploring the red sea . . . you fill your hat with rum &
heave it into the face of hailstone & not expect anything
new to be born . . . dogs wag their tails good-bye to you
& robin hood watches you from a stained glass window
. . . the opera singers will sing of YOUR forest & YOUR
cities & you shall stand alone but not make ceremony
. . . an old wrinkled prospector will appear & he will
NOT say to you 'dont be possessive! dont wish to be
remembered!' he will just be looking for his geiger
counter & his name wont be Moses & dont count your-
self lucky for not interfering – it is petty . . . do not count
yourself lucky

hi. just a note to say that ever
since the robbery, things've
kinda quiet down. altho theo's
kidnappers havent returned him
yet, dad got promoted to den
mother, so things are not all
going downhill/mom joined the
future fathers of alaska. really
likes it/ you oughta see little
dumbbell. he's nearly two now.
talks like a fish & is already
starting to look like a cigar/
see you on your birthday

big brother
Dunk

p.s. adolph got you a trick piece of puke which
you put on the table & just watch the
girls throw up

On Watching the Riot from a Filthy Cell or
(The Jailhouse Has No Kitchen)

standing on a bullet holed volkswagen, a bearded leprechaun & he's wearing a topless mafia cape – holding up some burning green stamps & he speaks out to the automobile graveyard 'four score & seven beers ago' & then he say 'etcetera' but his voice is drowned out by mickey mantle hitting a grand slam . . . the mayor of the city, with alka seltzer, climbs down from a limousine & asks 'who the hell is that leppo?' when a thousand angry tourists trample over him all donning baseball gloves & here comes the squad/ 'just who the hell are you?' speaks a garbage disposal 'i'm cole younger. gave my horse to the pony express, other'n that, i'm just like you' a rousing cheer & the ball crashes thru the fire box 'i work for the city. before i swat you, you'd best tell me your occupation' 'i'm an actor. tomorrow & tomorrow & tomorrow lights this petty grace from blow to blow like a poor stagehand pounding fury signifying nothing. oh romeo, romeo, wherefor fart thou? pretty good huh?' 'i work for the city, i'll trample you with my horse' 'wanna hear some oedipus?' but beneath the underground, Blind Andy Lemon & his friend, Lip, sing rabbit foot blues in spurs & light pullover design by Chung of paris – theyre standing in a fish bowl & everybody's throwing marbles at them . . . outside, however, after the tear gas disappears, we find that the leprechaun's got his

hand in a bandage & his beard's gone & the mayor, we
find out, is home making urgent phone calls to cardinal
spellman/ it has been a long time nite & everybody has
had lots of contact . . . i am ready for the cradle. the desert
is full of cattle

> sorry for not writing sooner. had
> to have some teeth pulled. finally
> read the great glaspy. helluva book
> just a helluva one. that cat sure
> tells it like it is. not much happening
> around here. Chucky tried to get the
> donkey to jump a fence. you can guess
> what happened there. sis got married
> to a real dog. i punched him out
> right away. that's all for now
>   see yuh on thanxgiving
>   Corky

Hopeless & Maria Nowhere

raggity ann daughter of brazos & teeth in the necklace-
ornery in the flesh & the border with the big laugh of bull-
fight ghost & LIBERACION & she, with the leather mother

thief & peeking DOS PASOS MAS ee & crazy ALLA
LUEGO UN RAYO & insane DE SOL & taking the
brothers to bed & to boredom – heat in every corner like
the silent parrot by SALA UN DIA & mad like a hatter
& the pig barker – maria ESTAS DESNUDA she digs holes
on my eyes the size of the moon while her father, he keeps
the hill warm & uncritical from deacons & the youngster
missionaries – maria sleep lightly PERO TE QUITARAS
cursing blond dynamite & TUS ROPAS . . . there is a
hatchet in maria's makeup & the spike driver moans, they
sound on her sink like the fornicating rattlesnake – friendly
on her nature & MARIA PORQUE LLORAS? & i give
you my twelve midnights & kick you with leapyear &
protect you from the crooked words & loyalty to the power
works & these little frogs with notebooks . . . maria
PORQUE TU RIES? freedom! she's the yardbird, the
constant & the old lady is made of marias & dogs yelping
& RECUERDOS oh how the furious yesterday, pyria
SON HECHOS laying bang DE ARCAICOS with simple
simon NADAS is still right now the poison nothing &
maria, me & you, we make up three TE QUIERO do not
churchize my nakedness – i am naked for you . . . maria,
she says i'm a foreigner. she picks on me. she pours salt on
my love

ok. so i shoot dope once in a
while. big deal. what's it got
to do with you? i'm telling you
mervin, if you dont lay off me,
i'm gonna rip you off some more
where that scar is, y'hear? like
i'm getting mad. next time you

call me that name in a public
cafeteria, i'm just gonna haul
off & kick you so you'll feel
it. like i aint even gonna get
angry. i'm just gonna let one
fly. fix you good

> better watch it
> The Law

A Confederate Poke into
King Arthur's Oakie

'. . . later i left the Casino
with one hundred & seventy
gulden in my pocket. it's
the absolute truth!'
> – fyodor dostoevsky

son of the vampire with his arm around betsy ross – he &
his society friends: Rain Man. Burt the Medicine. President
Plump. the Flower Lady & Baboon Boy . . . they all said
'happy new year, elmer & how's your wife, cecile?' & that
got them into the party free . . . once into the party, Burt

just stood around with a toothpick in the back of his neck watching for the doctor & tho the card game was something else in itself, Flower Lady lost her shirt & went into the bushes – who should come by but the little old wine maker trying to be helpful – 'get out of the picture' said Flower Lady 'you weren't at the party!' . . . the little old wine maker immediately took off his head & his belt & who do you think it turned out to be but fabian – 'i dont care how many tricks you can do, just get outa here!' . . . just then, this cable car on its way to washington came rumbling down the hill carrying crossword puzzles for everybody – Rain Man yelled 'watch out Flower Lady, there's an elephant coming!' but by this time she was singing auld lang syne with Baboon Boy, who'd snuck up, stuck a lead weight life jacket around fabian & threw him in the swimming pool – the Plump himself tried to give a warning but he was so drunk that he fell in a barrel & a tractor being driven by some dogs ran over him & dumped him into a garage . . . the world didnt stop for a second – it just blew up/ alfred hitchcock made the whole thing into a mystery & huntley & brinkley never slept for a week . . . the american flag turned green & andy clyde kept pestering about a back paycheck – every gymnasium in the world was picketed . . . son of the vampire, who got a divorce from betsy ross & now is with little red riding hood made it into january first carrying some empty stomachs – he & red, they got a job hiding door knobs & got paid good wages & like all people who decide not to go to any more parties, they put their money where their mouth is . . . & begin to eat it

translate this fact for me, dr.
blorgus: the fact is this: we

must be willing to die for
freedom (end of fact) now what
i wanna know about the fact is this: could
hitler have said it? de gaulle? pinocchio?
lincoln? agnes moorehead? goldwater? bluebeard?
the pirate? robert e. lee? eisenhower?
groucho smith? teddy kennedy? general franco?
custer? is it possible that jose melis
could have said it? perhaps donald o'connor?
i happen to be a library janitor, so could
you please clarify things a little for
me. thank you . . . by the way, if you do not
have a reply to me by this coming tuesday,
i will take it for granted that all these
forementioned people are all really the
same person . . . see you later. have to take
down a picture of lady godiva as the
mental students are touring here in an
hour . . .

                          considerately yours,
                          Popeye Squirm

Guitars Kissing & the Contemporary Fix

along black winds & white fridays, they wash out water & shriek of jungle & lenny immune to the mathematics, he, the greasy quack – the vagabond god . . . he plants flowers in their saddle bags & speaks of Jesus brave & graduating – tragedy, the broken pride, shallow & no deeper than comedy – bites his path, his noise, his shadow . . . resign from mind the heart of light & approve the doom, the bending & the farce of happy ending . . . those that would gas the memory & shut out the might of right, the sight of those defending & offending the blossom girls of the dark, pregnant, permanent & pale outlaw . . . fair gloria the bowlegged singer, the sign painter's bastard – joanne, raped by the town historian & silver dolly, devirginated at 12, by her father, a miner – maybelle with a chopped up arm from an uncle – doublejointed barbara, who grinds a compact into the face of a druggist & maureen, the jealous lover . . . none of them raking leaves – ratting on friends who are telephone operators or paying for the like of an e.e. cummings . . . none of them falling for the 'purr lost soul' talk of the hill-billy brawny gospel singer & lenny as the pilgrim angel – the crime but that he reigns in highway christ clothes, boots & a swagger . . . the lone shark wolf in a world where piemen castrate the dogs & cities for Du Pont, cat magazines & hiding in machines they chew gum, their seeds, their portraits . . . lenny leaves the woodchuck, the veteran of foreign war to his plymouth 6, his murder page – the Arms Bros chair & to his kidnapper & the radio siren/ the communists would call him lazy & the veteran calls him a bum & yo ho ho & a bottle of rum but he's nice to priests & dont tangle with the mayor's daughter 'n law . . . he wears silk & bows to yoyos, barbells & the strangers – he steals bow ties & heading for the north & waves to soldiers with amputated hands who picked up broken ashtray pieces & staying clear of muffled & exploding roosters, he pets ornaments & twin pipes/ there is a rhapsody to his toughness & he sure is warm & worthlessly wild.

> the deer thru the woods quite out of it
> all shall never be the slave but the target
> for military & freedom's legs having no
> substitute for death when sunday professor & the
> children come out, say 'watch it. you bound to
> stumble now!' & the lady in waiting just collapsing
> & asked if that's a threat or perhaps a friendly
> warning & the innocent coon being scraped on the
> table – liberty, an orphan sonnet, unwritten &
> having no eyes & needs, no defense & getting
> some glass in the veins – the conspiracy to kill
> the free & romantic to custom operating regularly
> on schedule & attacking now the once that run
> with no sidecar . . . go ahead, shoot! all you need
> is a license & a weak heart

thru the braided hair & loafing beer can beach of wood – brains of the roadhouse & panel trucks filled with cucumber funk, jim beam sweating & lords & ladies in the rear view mirror – humanity in the gang bang mood & yodeling swimmers – the kinks from strike town & itty bitty pretty one lapping up the crankcase rotgut & lenny laughing in a fake sombrero & the jugglers trying to smother the queers & the girls from big city & panoramic way, you found lenny, the dog catcher killer & motorcycle saint – you either love him or hate him – attracting the filthy mamas, Tom the Wretched, Mike the Bull & Hazel, the pornographic back slapper . . . lenny can take the bad out of you & leave you all good & he can take the good out of you & leave you all bad/ if you think youre smart & know things, lenny plays with your head & he contradicts everything youve been taught about people/ he is not in the history books & he either makes you glad to be you or he makes you hate to be you . . . you know he's some kind of robber yet you trust him & you cannot ignore him

. . . the lion's den then, & anchors away & you remember the table – the hopped up table of worldly wiggies & unpatriotics & the slut madonna with her squatter's rights & everybody sexy & picking on the car thieves & some bumbling sacred cow telling how he marched right in & trimmed this chicken just like that but when peter pan of the throttle bums gets up to go someplace, it's growling & wondering & sentimental because you know he never does – while gloria talks of the fish in her finger with her hair dyed pink & speaking of tomorrow, calling it sunday & the engine slams & really slams into first gear – & it sounds like john lee hooker coming & oh Lordy louder like a train . . . the punchdrunk sailor with a scar below his nose suddenly slaps & kicks little sally & makes her let go of the bottoms of his dungarees & you Know he knows something's happening & it aint the ordinary kind of sound that you can see so clearly & carrrrrashhhhh & a technicolor passion of berserk & napoleonic & suicide & lenny vanishes in the daytime & a bridge girder all lonesome & gone & the trumpets play what theyve always been taught to play in time of emergency – Babylon's sweetheart & the redblooded boy oozing all over & shock, the defunct rockabilly in a blindfold – dissolve into the motherland for touch & kneeling to instinct, gypsies & into the most northernmost forest he can find

. . . a roaring free for all is witnessed later between as follows: rabbit seller, who, because he lives in a room where the rain continues to fall thru the chimney, always has a chronic cough & is constantly in an al capone type mood – call him White Man/ the ex faggot g.i., who now transports dummies from macy's to yankee stadium & whose ears always bleed in heavy weather – call him Black Man/ the hatcheck girl with a glass eye, whose father taught her how to walk exactly like P.T. Barnum & now she discovers it means nothing – call her Audience/ the candle stick maker, with a mouthful of plastic & his pockets full of used matches – call him Reward/ the bathing beauty who wears a turban full of meatballs – call her Success/ the tug of war rope & a holy bell – boom & the pumphouse guardian stepping out of his coocoo & saying 'words are objects! sight is ego! did any of you freaks ever know a lenny? i can remember his last name . . .' & then some vigilante, he say 'get back in your clock! you ever heard of lions one, christians nothing?' & after sending hitler out to murder the poor guardian, he jumps back into the christians & clocks & all types of mink, milk & vitamin C – grannies in titepants & barechested undertakers goosing preachers wearing egg cartons & U.N. generals in

bathrobes & their feet stuck in bongo drums & three
million jealous teachers in used roy acuff strings all
flunking little de gaulles & prison choruses bursting &
singing hallaluyah . . . everybody even Good St. Doc &
the bird scientist sucking scruples & nipples & trying to
hide their shit . . . everybody saying 'disaster!' & pointing
& examining hanging clowns & making reports & going
'gah gah' at dead pontiacs & babies in Lorca graves . . .
the tax collector stealing everybody's useless sacrifice &
H.G. Wells unheeded . . . Lulu the Smith having a heart
attack at the birth of a black angel & john brown, Luke
the snob & Achilles all reaching for the Flying Saucer . . .
one day, the day of the Tambourines, the astronaut, Micky
McMicky, will remove a thumb from his mouth – say 'go
to hell' while lenny i'm sure is already in a resentful heaven

dear dropout magazine,
gentlemen:
i understand that you are currently
putting a book together about
blacklisted or blackheaded artists or something.
if it is the former, then i shall have to
recommend that you place jerry lee lewis first
an foremost. if it is the latter, then i shall
have to recommend that you contact the american
medical society to discover the exact worth of
such an undertaking
                    in all respects, i remain
                    a rabble rouser from the mountains
                    Zeke the Cork

Advice to Hobo's Model

paint your shoes delilah – ye walk on white snow where a nosebleed would disturb the universe . . . down these narrow alleys of owls an flamenco guitar players, jack paar an other sex symbols are your prizes – check into the bathrooms where bird lives for when he comes flying out with a saber in his wing – a country music singer by his side – digesting a carrier pigeon . . . ye just might change your style of fornicating, sword swallowing – ye just might change your way of sleeping on nails – paint your shoes the color of the ghost mule – the paper tiger's teeth are made of aluminum – youve a long time to Babylon – paint your shoes, delilah – paint them with a sponge

look! like i told you before, it doesnt
matter where it's at! there's no such
thing. it's where it's not at that you
gotta know. so what if tony married his
mother! what's it got to do with your life?
i really have no idea why youre so unhappy.
perhaps you ought to change your line of
work. you know. like how long can someone
of your caliber continue to paint pencil
sharpeners . . . see you next summer, good to
know you're off the wagon.

prematurely yours,
Funka

A Blast of Loser Take Nothing

jack of spades – vivaldi of the coin laundry – wearing a
hipster's dictionary – we see him brownnosing around the
blackbelts & horny racing car drivers – dashing to & fro
like a frightened uncle remus . . . on days that he gets no
mail, he rises early, sticks paper up the pay phones & cons
the bubble gum machines . . . 'the world owes me a living'
he says to his half-hawaiian cousin, the half-wit, joe the
head who is also planning to marry a folksinger next month
– 'round & round, old joe clark' is being recited from the
steps of the water & light building as jack ambles by with
a case full of plastic bubbles – things look well for him:
he can imitate cary grant pretty good. he knows all the
facts why mabel from utah walked out on horace, the light-
ingman from Theatre Altitude, he has even stumbled onto
a few hairy secrets of mrs. Cunk, who sells fake blisters at
the world's fair – plus being able to play a few foreign
legion songs on the yoyo & always managing to look like
a grapefruit in case of emergency . . . he brags about his
collection of bruises & corks & the fact that he pays no
attention to the business world. he would rather show his
fear of the bomb & say what have you done for freedom
than to praise an escaped mental patient who pisses on the
floor of junior's delicatessen – jack of spades, with his axe,
the record player, with his companion, the menu. & his
destination, a piece of kleenex – never touches the cracks
on the sidewalk – 'jack' says his other cousin, Bodeguard,
half danish & half surfer, 'how come you always act like
Crazy, jackie gleason's friend? i mean wow! aint there

enough sadness in the world?' jack walks by in a flash –
he wears ear plugs – from the steps of the water & light
building, the band, after knocking all the juice out of their
horns, begin to play on my papa . . . jack, shocked, takes
a second look, raises his hand in a nazi salute, a woodsman,
walking by with an axe, drops it, a D.A.R. woman flies
off the handle. looks at jack. says 'in some places, you'd
be arrested for obscenity' she doesn't even hear the band
. . . she falls down a sidewalk crack/ the band leader, paying
no attention, does a slight curtsy, sneezes. points his wand
at the classical guitar . . . a street cleaner bumps into jack
& says & i quote 'o.k. so i bumped into you. i don't even
care. i got me a little woman at home. i know a good radi-
ator down the block. man, i aint never gonna starve. would
you like to buy a pail?' jack, amazed, rearranges his collar
& heads off to the bell telephone hour. which is located
beyond the next cop car . . . he passes a hot dog stand. a
sauerkraut hits him in the face . . . the band is playing
malaguena sale-rosa – the D.A.R. woman pops out of the
sidewalk, hears the band, screams, starts doing the jerk.
the street cleaner steps on her . . . jack hasn't eaten all day.
his mouth tastes funny – he has his unpublished novel in
his hand – he wants to be a star – but he gets arrested
anyway

hi y'all. not much new happening.
sang at the vegetarian convention
my new song against meat. everybody
dug it except for the plumbers neath
the stage. this one little girl,
fresh out of college & i believe
president of the Dont Stomp Out the

Cows division of the society. she tried
to push me into one of the plumbers.
starts a little chaos going, but you
know me, i didnt go for that not one
little bit. i say 'look baby, i'll sing
for you & all that, but just you dont
go pushing me, y'hear—' i understand
that theyre not gonna invite me back
cause they didnt like the way i came on
to the master of ceremony's old lady, all
in all, i'm making it tho. got a new song
against a cigarette lighters. this matchbook
company offered me free matches for the rest
of my life, plus my picture on all the
matchbooks, but you know me, it'd take a
helluva lot more'n that before i'd sell out –
see you around nomination time

> your fellow rebel
> kid tiger

making love on maria's friend

yawn to foxy queenie school teacher – gone, decatur &
entering the pink highway – your black mongrel vagabond,
your rat from Delphi – now he shall tattle on your nauseous

bra – your hair in chains & speak TU CAMINO while your El Paso ideals, they celebrate ES TERCIOPELO they leave your gruesome body – your structure falling, you listen for a lazy siren & some young Spaniard to buy your wounds, your pregnant drawl . . . yawn to queenie of the Goya painting seeking poor Homer QUEDATE CONMIGO while the dikes break & count your number & Baby Mean crying NO PREDENDAS while author Fritz from your industrial south yelling what's this all about & get the hell home, queenie & you, queenie, the spider – the sweat web's got you – you beg your arms to move – you pray to be righteous – you look for postcards & teddy bears for payoffs – the partisans, they laugh CON TUS PIERNAS & the boys with brown rags, they whisper of the bust & already they have Leo the Sneak & Doc's gonna have to leave by noon – St. Willy hides in the pawnshop PARA QUEENIE you need not fear & nobody's chasing – you want to be held LA ERRONEA DAMA & dig into your purse – forget your pupils & pay for your partner & botheration – the shadow of your boss, it is your felony – author Fritz would like to suck your toe – your holiday be gone soon & vanishing like your life LA CHOTA the grass cuts your feet & Socrates' Prison is your goal AHI VIENEN you are the wrong lady – you threaten nobody – spend your money on health food & you shall be run over by a truck – they'll put a tag on you – send you home to Fritz – Fritz will cry for a week & marry your nurse – the dikes will curl their mouths but you'll still be the wrong one TODOS SON DE LA CHOTA live now . . . live before you board your Titanic – reach out, Queenie, reach out – feel for equal saggy skin & believe this dark playboy licking ink from your notebook – see the cages & screaming ghosts & you with the gall to think that ruins are buildings . . . take your bloody glands & medallion & make love once freely – it means nothing so wear a top hat – travel on a slow ship back to your guilt, your pollution, the kingdom of your blues

hi. watcha doing? how's the new religion?
feel any different? gave it up myself. just
couldnt make all the auctions and frankly,
i's running out of bread. you know how it
is, like about that little old lady in the
back building all the time pointing telling
me that God is watching. you know, like for a
while there, i's scared to take a shit. anxious
to get together with you. i know you dont wear
bow ties anymore but i'm interested in other
aspects of your new faith too. by the way, are
you still in the keyhole business? cant wait
to talk to you

                                    bye,
                                    your buddy,
                                    Testy

Note to the Errand Boy
as a Young Army Deserter

wonder why granpa just sits there & watches yogi bear?
wonder why he just sits there & dont laugh? think about
it kid, but dont ask your mother. wonder why elvis presley
only smiles with his top lip? think about it kid, but dont
ask your surgeon. wonder why the postman with one leg
shorter'n the other kicked your dog so hard? think about
it kid, but dont ask any mailman. wonder who ronald
reagan talked to about the foreign situation? think about
it kid, but dont ask any foreigners. wonder why the
mechanic, whose wife shot herself with a gun she got from
his best friend, hates castro so much? wonder why castro
hates rock n roll? think about it kid, but dont ask no roll.
wonder how much the man who wrote white christmas
made? think about it, but dont ask no made. wonder what
bobby kennedy's really got against jimmy hoffa? think
about it, but dont ask no bobby. wonder why frankie shot
johnny? go ahead, wonder, but dont ask your neighbor . . .
wonder who the carpet baggers are? think, but dont ask
no carpet. wonder why youre always wearing your
brother's clothes? think about it kid, but dont ask your
father. wonder why general electric says that the most
important thing for a family to do is stick together? think
about it, kid, but don't ask no together . . . wonder what
paydirt is? go ahead, wonder . . . wonder why the other
boys wanna beat you up so bad? think about it, kid, but
dont ask nobody

yes. ok. i guess youre a pumpkin.
yes, it's true i referred to you as 'that
chinese girl' you have a right to
be angry. but what i want to know
is just what have you got against
the chinese anyway?

>maybe we can still work
>it out
>properly yours,
>prince goulash

Taste of Shotgun

the roar of our engines promises us cover – we wear choking
pants & are slaves to appetite – we get stoned on joan
crawford & form teeming colonies & die of masculine
conversation . . . Marcellus, wearing khaki when madness
struck him, immediately filed suit against an illegitimate son
belonging to someone else – Josie said everybody at the trial
came with a blowgun . . . Tom Tom made Melodius hate
him, then jumped from a window – we are all alike & place
scorpions neatly in our insides – we take pills thru the ass
– we praise faggot missionaries & throw homosexuals into
phenomenon gutters . . . in the winter a blackface musician
announces he is from Two Women – he spends his free

time trying to peel the moon & he's here to collect his eight
cent stamp – Marguerita the pusher, wheeling a cartful of
Thursday up Damaen's Row yelling 'cockles & muscles',
kills him for getting in the way of her appetite . . . the
rewards are few on Chemical Isle – little girls hide perfume
up their shrimps & there are no giants – the warmongers
have stolen all our german measles & are giving them to
the doctors to use as bribes – i stayed awake for three hours
last nite with Pearl – she claimed to have walked by a
rooming house i once lived in – we had nothing in common,
me & Pearl – i shared her boredom & had nothing to give
her – i was drunk & entertained myself . . . we wish to
make journeys & use everything excpt our feet & we meet
tongue tied broken vulgar geeks with gorilla handshakes
& drunken Hercules waits for us on our beds & we must
salute him & he says that the new helicopters have arrived
& 'this is your geek' & 'you will take your orders from
him' yes the rewards are few here but there are no oaths
to take nor mental strokes – excpt for the self conscious
insanity brought in by hunters with radios wearing reli-
gious clothes, all goes well . . . Angola being bombed this
morning, i right now am happy with nausea – my head is
suffocating – i am gazing into the big dipper with silver
buttoned blouse in my nostrils – i'm glad Marguerita's all
right – i Do feel expensive

    i am leaving my kid on your
    doorstep, if youre so hot, you'll
    see that he gets taken care of.
    after all, he's your kid too. i
    expct to see him in about twenty
    years, so you better do a good

job. i am going into the mountains
to find work. i am taking along
the food. remember luv, keep the
stove clean & watch the gas tank
                    yours
                    louie louie

Mae West Stomp (A Fable)

train goes by every nite the same old time & he, same old
man, sits looking into a rosary which reads 'i told you so'
while rocking back & forth thinking about his eldest son,
Hambone, who's in jail for life – buying beer for the kids
& murdering the grocer with a pocket comb – this same
old man, with nothing but a bathtub full of memories
consisting of: a few Baby Huey for President buttons – a
deck of cards with the aces missing – some empty deodorant
bottle – a pamphlet of egyptian slogans – three pant legs
that dont match & a hollow lynch rope . . . sits in a candy
wrapper chair muttering day in court – day in court – i'll
get it yet – my day in court – a dapper young gentleman
with chapped lips rubbed them on the old man's neck today
– the little old man is planning revenge just as the same old
time train shakes his whistler's mother painting off the wall
& it gooses him to . . . day in court – i'll get it yet –

yesterday was not so good either – a fox left him in a clump of mud & some little pest let him have it right in the kisser with a mixture of bamboo, barley & rotten ice cream – there he sits wishing he could get thru to the president – the little old man's bowels ache so he opens the window to breathe some good fresh air – he inhales deeply – there is a line full of wet underwear – used tires – dirty bed sheets – hats – chicken feathers – an old watermelon – paper plates – some other garments – johnny drumming wind – an indian, passing thru on his way to st. louis, is standing neath the old man's window – 'amazing' he says as he looks up & sees all this stuff on the clothesline suddenly get sucked into a hole . . . next day, the rent collector comes to get the rent – finds that the old man has disappeared & that the room's full of garbage – the lady who owns the clothes-line, she reports theft to the robber department – 'all my valuables have been stolen' – she mutters to the inspector – the train still goes by at the same old time & johnny drumming wind, he gets picked up for vagrancy – the rent collector looks around – steals a broken coocoo 'i think i'll give it to my wife' he says – his wife, who is six feet tall & wears a fez, & who, at the minute, by weird circum-stance, is riding by on that same old time train – all in all, not much happens in chicago

    i'm not saying that books are
    good or bad, but i dont think
    youve ever had the chance to find
    out for yourself what theyre all
    about – ok, so you used to get B's
    in the ivanhoe tests & A minuses
    in the silas marners . . . then you

wonder why you flunked the hamlet
exams – yeah well that's because one
hoe & one lass do not make a spear –
the same way two wrongs do not make
a throng – now that youve been thru
life, why dont you try again . . . you
could start with a telephone book –
wonder woman – or perhaps catcher in
the rye – theyre all the same & everybody
has their hat on backwards thru the
stories

see you at the docks
helpfully yours,
Sir Cringe

Black Nite Crash

aretha in the blues dunes – Pluto with the high crack laugh
& rambling aretha – a menace to president as he was jokingly
called – go – yea! & the seniority complex disowning you
. . . Lear looking in the window dangerous & dragging a
mountain & you say 'no i am a mute' & he says 'no no i've
told the others you were Charlie Chaplin & now you must
live up to it – you must!' & aretha saying 'split Lear – none
of us got the guts for infinity – take your driving-wheel &

split . . . & aretha next – she's got these hundred Angel
Strangers all passing thru saying 'i will be your Shakti &
your outlaw kid – pick me – pick me please – ah c'mon pick
me' & aretha faking her intestinal black soul across all the
fertile bubbles & whims & flashy winos – Jinx, Poet Void
& Scary Plop all skipping to hell with their bunnies where
food is cheaper & warmer & Nucleur Beethoven screaming
'oh aretha – i shall be your voodoo doll – prick me – let's
make somebody hurt – draw on me whoever you wish! ah
pretty please! my bastard frame – my slimy self – penetrate
unto me – unto me!' Scholar, his body held together by
chiclets – raw beans & slaves of days gone by – he storms
in from the road – his pipe nearly eaten 'look! she burps of
reality' & but he's not even talking to anybody – a moth
flies out of his pocket & Void, the incredible fall apart
reminds you once more of america with the dotted line –
useless motive – the moral come on & silver haired men
hiding in the violin cases . . . on a mound of phosphorus &
success stands the voluptuous coyote eagle – he holds a half
dollar – an anchor sways across his shoulders 'good!' says
Nucleur Beethoven 'good to see there are some real birds
around' 'that's no bird – that's just a thief – he's building an
outhouse out of stolen lettuce!' signs aretha – Sound of
Sound – who really doesnt give a damn about real birds or
outhouses or any Nucleur Beethoven – approval, complaints
& explanations – they all frighten her – she has no flaws in
her trumpet – she knows that the sun is not a piece of her

the audio repairman stumbles
thru the door with 'sound is sacred –
so come in & talk to us' written on
the back of his shirt

Hostile Black Nite Crash

on this abandoned roof or pagoda stool they place you &
you hear voices saying things like 'titen 'm up Joe – keep
'm titened up' & then Orion looking evil & he wipes you
off & keeps you clean & Familiar Face himself 'i heard you
been eating some eggs? any truth to that?' & Orion licking
his flesh & trouble in mind blues & shades of fire hydrants
. . . YOU – the fire hydrant & Beau Geste, a fire hydrant
– failures completely & walking to Gibraltar & trying to
find your energy – get your kicks & shadow box your
language . . . Faust from the garden – Emancipation Anne,
who looks like a hungarian deer & Chump with a brain
like an iceberg all imitating Africa . . . Dead Lover who
hitchhikes & brags & says he's going to Carthage & he
keeps repeating 'when i die' but then his mind goes black
& blue & methodist butter erupting & Twinkle Clown with
arabic lettering on his forehead wanting everybody to expe-
rience his fright 'you must experience my fright to be my
friend!' so says he to Lucy Tunia, whose vegetarian legs
shine like mahogany & who comforts Twinkle Clown in
his fits when he has no harem . . . Zing & Orion stutters
& coughs & SHAZAMMM – the opium ghost neath the
ferris wheel – on the side of the highway – where nobody
can stop – where he can cause no trouble – where the show
must go on . . . this is where He wishes to die – He wishes
to die in the midst of cathedral bells – He wishes to die
when the tornadoes strike the roofs & stools 'so much for
death' he will say when he dies

the newsboy comes in the back door –
his big toe sticks thru his shoe – he
carries a piece of peeling with a
number on it – he makes a phone call –
then he blows his nose

Unresponsible Black Nite Crash

the united states is Not soundproof – you might think that
nothing can reach those tens of thousands living behind
the wall of dollar – but your fear Can bring in the truth
. . . picture of dirt farmer – long johns – coonskin cap –
strangling himself on his shoe – his wife, tripping over
the skulls – her hair in rats – their kid is wearing a scor-
pion – the scorpion wears glasses – the kid, he's drinking
gin – everybody has balloons stuck into their eyes – that
they will never get a suntan in mexico is obvious – send
your dollar today – bend over backwards – or shut your
mouths forever

the bully comes in – kicks the newsboy
you know where – & begins ripping away
at the audio repairman's shirt

Electric Black Nite Crash

nature has made the young West Virginia miners not want
to be miners but rather get this '46 Chevy – no money down
– take to Geneva . . . hunting for the likes of escape & Lord
Buckley & Sherlock Holmes about to be his mother turning
to Starhole the Biology Amazon saying 'i dont want to be
my mother!' & e.e. cummings – spell it right – wrapping
his leftover chicken bones in a pig tail belonging to Bronx
Baby No. 2 & she thinks the world's coming to an end &
tries to organize a rally & her 320 pound Frenchman who
sticks his tongue out at her father – he dont want no part
of it – 'i dont wanna go to no San Quentin! i'm not a crim-
inal – i'm a foreigner & i cant help it if you dig e.e. cummings
but me – like ah said – i'm just a foreigner' & she throws
all these leftover chicken bones into his face & some celeb-
rities passing by – they witness the whole thing & take
down the serial numbers . . . Mona carries a lone ranger
advertisement on her left front breast – Mona's cousin – this
320 pound Frenchman – he resembles Arthur Conan Doyle
. . . Mona – she resembles a sexy Buddha & always looks
like she's standing over the Golden Gate . . . she dont dig
e.e. cummings – she digs Fernando Lamas – i am on a black
train going west – there is no aretha on the desert – just –
if you want – memories of aretha – but aretha teaches not
to depend on memory – there is no aretha on the desert

    the stripper comes in wearing an
    engagement ring – she asks for lemonade,

but says she'll settle for a sandwich –
the newsboy grabs her – yells 'lord have
mercy'

Somebody's Black Nite Crash

from entire Mexico & gay innocence once comes Satan of
Autumn – from the gentleness & barbarian bebop & lone-
some rooms where you must put a nickel in the parking
meter – into the arms of notorious daughters – daughters
who get social poems published in bazaar & fashion maga-
zines & wonder of adventure – beer barrel polkas & eat
goofballs 'why didnt HUAC get custer?' say some 'how
did robert burns escape hitler is what i'd like to know!'
say the smarter ones – all the hipster T-bone heads & wheel
chair Marxists wishing to be in Kansas City '51 & Satan
of Autumn & his friend, I DONT KNOW YOU, gnawing
farts in the farmlands & coming back & telling everybody
& then I DONT KNOW YOU finally coming to the
conclusion 'what good's it all to tell everybody about
anything – they all got alibis?' & then Montana coming &
Aztec Landlords themselves – their atomic fag bars being
looted & Bishops disguised as chocolate prisoners & the
empty Barbary Coast haunted houses where the bureau-
crats – the dreamy Huxley hanger oners – the New Awake

with money & no place else to go & the ex cop who writes verse & thinks of himself as a salami & Gabby – the crippled horror from Telegraph Avenue but who wants to hear of this – who really wants to hear of this? 'who wants to hear anything? we just a part of a generation! just one mangy grubby part!' said I DONT KNOW YOU one day to Satan & it was autumn 'you mean like the hula hoop happening?' 'no – like the crucifixion happening!' 'like the Modern beat?' 'like the beat of a peach tree' . . . both Satan & I DONT KNOW YOU – they skip thru the New York race track – all the typical renaissances & a blond that looks like ezra pound & they go right into Summer – without winter – seeing them so unsuffered, Lu with a crew cut, one of the chicks that write the big fat writings – her mouth hangs open – some beggar comes out of his hovel & hangs a hair from her lip – a streetcar crashes . . . but all in all – nobody really cares

> the chamber of commerce all come in –
> each member carrying hand grenades –
> everything turns into blood – excpt for
> the jukebox, a stranger wearing a——
> calendar, & a postcard of a greek
> building . . . which the owner of the
> place has left on top of the radiator
> by mistake/ the play now begins . . . it
> is all in the past . . . i will not be
> so insulting as to write it for you

Seems Like a Black Nite Crash

between the shrieking mattress in the kitchen & Time, a mysterious weekly – Tao – a fingertip on his chin, his knees knocking together – Tao – he shows the inside of his mouth to a column of faces 'does this mean you must take a nap today?' & Phil Silvers eating a banana – he is inside of the column of faces – Tao is quiet & Phil pokes Duff the Hero – a miser from the Aegean Sea – a vast desert in his head – he has plenty of self confidence & lets yokels test bombs in his brain – 'love is a ghost thing' says Duff 'it goes right thru you' Tao strains – he looks almost pornographic 'some tonsils!' says Phil, who now wears long suspenders & tells Duff to keep up the self confidence 'self confidence is deceiving' says Mr. O'toole – a husband of questionable virtue 'it gives people without balls a sense of virility' 'does your wife own a cow?' says Phil, who has now turned into an inexpensive Protestant ambassador from Nebraska & who speaks with a marvelous accent 'what do you mean does my wife own a cow?' 'are you from Chicago then?' asks the ambassador . . . Tao's face – meanwhile – becomes so big – it disappears 'where'd he go?' says Duff – who's not so much of a hero anymore but rather a jolly youth that hates degenerates & is supposed to be in school anyway . . . Mr. O'toole – falls out of his chair 'i must find some railroad tracks – i must put my ear to the tracks – i must listen for a train' – the column of faces – all together now – a munching chorus 'DONT GET KILLED NOW' – repeat – 'dont get killed now' . . . yes & between this mattress shrieking & that mysterious weekly lay the slave counties – Doris Day gone & Pacific fog – a Studebaker in twilight – crash – & breaking down the honkytonk doors & strange left handed moonmen – from Arkansas & Texas & vagabonds with girlie magazines from Reed College – cellars & Queens – they all shouting 'watch me Tao – watch me – i'm high – watch me now!' . . . that lonesome feeling – paralyzing – that lonesome feeling – or aretha – my mama didnt raise no fool – i have nothing new to add to that feeling . . . slide on vomit – better'n working with a shovel – Reject – God Bless Holy Phantomism & damn the farewell parties – statistic books – the politicians . . . the column of faces – all together now – raising the flag & staring up to a hole in it – chanting 'it's halloween! can Tao come out & play?' – getting no reaction & shouting louder – all in unison now – 'IT'S HALLOWEEN . . . CAN TAO COME OUT & PLAY?'

> give up – give up – the ship is lost: go
> back to san bernardino – stop trying to
> organize the crew – it's every man for
> himself – are you a man or a self? when
> the coast guard gets there, stand up
> proudly & point – dont be a hero – everybody's
> a hero – be different – dont be a conformist –
> forget about all those sea shanties – just
> stand up & say 'san bernardino' in a deep
> monotone . . . everybody will get the message
> your benefactor
Smoky Horny

Chug A Lug—Chug A Lug
Hear Me Hollar Hi Dee Ho

he was propped in the crutch of an oak tree – looking down
– singing 'there's a man going round taking names' indeed
– i nod howdy – he nods howdy back 'well he took my
mother's name – lef' me there in pain' i, who am holding
a glass of sand in one hand & a calf's head in the other –
i look up & say 'are you hungry?' & he say 'there's a man
going round taking names' & i say 'good nuff' & keep
walking – his voice rings thru the valley – it sounds like a
telephone – it is very disturbing – 'you need anything up
there?' – i'm going to town' he shakes his head 'well he
took my sister's name & i aint never been the same' 'right-
o' i say – tie my shoelace & keep walking – then i turn &
say 'if you need any help getting down, just you come to
town & tell me' he doesn't even hear – 'well he took my
uncle's name & you know he wasnt to blame' 'groovy' i
say & continue my way to town . . . it couldnt've been
more'n a few hours later when i happened to be passing
by again – in the spot where the tree was, a lightbulb factory
now stood – 'did there used to be a guy here in a tree?' i
yelled up to one of the windows – 'are you looking for
work?' was the reply . . . it was then when i decided that
marxism did not have all the answers

why are you so frightened of
being embarrassed? you spend a lot of
time on the toilet dont you? why

dont you admit it? why are you so
embarrassed to be frightened?

> your uncle
> Matilda

Paradise, Skid Row & Maria Briefly

fatty Aphrodite's mama – i bend to you . . . & with sex
mad eternity at my vegetable shadow – i, wiping my hands
on the horse's neck – the horse burping & you of the
Indiana older brother – he who whips you with his belt &
you who does not look for reason to your torture & i want
your horizontal tongue – within Reflex – the perfect doom
& these cruel nitemares where brickmasons introduce me
to hideous connections & Marx Brothers grunting NO
QUIERO TU SABIDURIA & your thighs be half awake
& me so Sick so Sick of these lovers in Biblical roles – 'so
youre out to save the world are you? you impostor – you
freak! youre a contradiction! youre afraid to admit youre
a contradiction! youre misleading! you have big feet & you
will step on yourself all the people you mislead will pick
you up! you have no answers! you have just found a way
to pass your time! without this thing, you would shrivel
up & be nothing – you are afraid of being nothing – you
are caught up in it – it's got you!' i am so Sick of Biblical

people – they are like castor oil – like rabies & now i wish
for Your eyes – you who does not talk any business &
supplies my mind with blankness QUIERO TUS OJOS
& your laughing & your slavery . . . there be no drunken
risk – i am an intimate Egyptian – say good-bye to the
marine

> hi – just arrived – terrible trip – this
> little man carrying a white mouse
> stared at me the whole way – jesus he
> was a handsome man – are there any good
> lawyers around? will look you up shortly –
> have to eat first
>
> > sincerely yours,
> > Froggy

A Punch of Pacifist

Peewee the Ear, whose mouth looks like a credit card –
him & Jake the Flesh – along with Sandy Bob from Pecos
– theyre leading the white elephant to water somewhere
between wichita falls & el camino real – it's late in the day
& no word from Saigon is in yet – along comes jerry mc
boing-boing's daughter – Liza the Blimp – riding on a two

dollar bill belonging to Goose John Henry, negro medi-
cine man from Denver, who plays folk songs for kicks &
speaks french for a living – onward then when Brown Dan,
the creep cop – who likes to kill bullfrogs & whose boss
keeps saying 'he's got a bad knee but you oughta see him
run, babe, you oughta see 'm run & chase them little chink
lovers when they come down the river' – anyway Brown
Dan – he comes snooping for the strangers with his flunky
known simply as Little Stick, who carries a burnt hat pin
& two pieces of kotex in case of emergency . . . they meet
up with the crew at a clearing resembling a fisherman's
dwarf . . . Jim Ghandi, the welder, is overlooking from his
window – & yells something like 'aw reet ye sons a vermits
– draw ye now or shut ye mouths frever' just as the chick
spreads her legs into the intersection & lets loose with the
bumble seed grease, but nobody sneezes – she begins to
yell about who her father is, but this doesnt work either
. . . her fat two dollar bill falls dead from a bullet – 'the
flag of tex's ass is upon ye' screams Jim Ghandi & the chick
immediately takes to the hills – Peewee drops his cookies
as up drives an XKE with Sandy Bob's cousin, Sandy Slim,
who shows everybody his pictures of Nasser & says 'hold
it boys, i know all about these things – i used to work in
the edsel factory' taking advantage of the confusion, Little
Stick steals the white elephant . . . nobody notices – not
even Brown Dan, who by this time is busy beating Jake
the Flesh to death with a hacksaw – all in all, the situation
in viet nam is very disturbing

        who wants to be noticed anyway? only you,
        who believes what suits you, could speak
        so badly of thelonius baker – what'd he

ever do to you anyway besides get his
name in the papers? dont you know that
everybody wants to pick a moron for you –
dont concern yourself with all this
pettiness – it will all pass – think big –
youve seen the sign – all in all, tho,
youre a pretty good guy – stay clean –
dont waste your money on haircuts – see you
at the drugstore

                              your highness,
                              Gumbo the Hobo

Sacred Cracked Voice
& the Jingle Jangle Morning

go on – flutter ye mystic ballad – ah haunting & Tokay
jittery ye be like the mad pulse – the mad pulse of child –
the children of ring around the rosy & wandering poets
over India – the jugglers who call you by the wrong name
& title you wounded kitten – it is that easy for they know
no fairy tales . . . in the modal tuning – a pontiac is parked
without a leg to stand on – Plague the Kid – crusading in
the blues dimension, he – hitchhiking the pontiac –
brooding over the highway & searching for Joker – or

perhaps the devil's eight drummer 'down with enthusiasm!' says Plague 'it is all temporary! away with it!' & Lord Randall playing with a quart of beer – Fanny Blair dragging a judge – Willy Moore, a shoemaker, who counts his thumbs with a switchblade along with Sir James, the dunce, who wears a stovepipe when he goes out on the town – Matty Groves, who secretly at midnight tries to chop down the church steeple with Edward, who cuts hedges for his wages & last but not least – Barbara Allen – she smuggles Moroccan cinders into Brooklyn twice a month & she wears a sheet – she takes many penicillin shots 'anything temporary can be used for money reasons' says Plague & all these people – call them what you will – they believe him – yesterday i talked to Abner for forty minutes – he, Abner – cursed out East Texas, tomatoes & tin pan alley – he didnt talk to me – he talked into a mirror – i did not have the courage to crash or shatter myself . . . when i left him, i met Puff – Puff had nothing but bad words for unemployment, Wrigley's Spearmint & Rabelais – i slapped myself in the face – he told me i was crazy & my only regret being that i could not fart thru my mouth – i walked away into a dimestore . . . what i speak of is the crazy unspeakable microphone & great flower celebration – it is not phony vision but rather friendly dark – behold the dark – your strength – the darkness 'the matrimony of self & spinal dream' says Plague the Kid & we buy him a boxcar – Hysterical – melody in the Hysterical – as opposed to the music which offers every sound to make life existable excpt that of silence . . . Houdini & the rest of the ordinary people taking down puckered Jesus posters out there on 61 highway – Midas putting them back up – in the throne sinks Cleo – she sinks because she's fat . . . this land is your land & this land is my land – sure – but the world

is run by those that never listen to music anyway – 'enthu-
siasm is music which needs a flashlight to be heard' so says
Plague

> sorry to say baby but you ARE hung up
> arent you? you know like suppose everybody
> DOES tell you youre like sabatchead
> dajapeeled . . . you know what happened to him
> after everybody read him – yeah he went
> right up on the shelf . . . let me know if
> you could use a horse tamer or a good
> worried mind . . .
>
> your meatman
> Shorty Cookie

Flunking the Propaganda Course

strange men with belly trouble & their pin up girls: zelda
rat – crooked betty & volcano the leg – here they come –
theyre popped out & theyve been seen crying in the chapel
– their friend, who says that everybody cries alot – he's the
congressional one & carries the snapshots – his name is
Tapanga Red – known in L.A. as Wipe'M Out – he coughs
alot – anyway they walk in – it's very early & they ask for

black mongrels apiece – jenny says 'why not roll 'm?' 'theyre cops!' says a little boy who just climbed a mountain & who's learned how to smell in the circus – jenny retires to the pinball machine – steam getting thicker – zelda rat asks for second black mongrel – please make it hot – one of the men, he dangles a watch in front of her face 'it's late – zeld babe – it's late' & zelda's face turns into a measle & she says 'i'm allergic' – a ringing sound & she say 'oh look – that girl over there is getting free balls' – trying to get jenny's attention, one of the men, he asks 'anything bothering you?' jenny replies 'yes – whatever happened to Orval Faubus?' & the man quickly drops the subject – his eye swollen he pushes one of the hot mongrels down poor zelda's dress – asks now does she wanna nother one – everybody breaks into stitches excpt someone who's talking to a window & jenny, who's busy racking up balls . . . the man who looks like an adam's apple – i think he belongs to crooked betty – he goes thru his stool – volcano – she wraps him in the national insider – everybody reads him – jenny tilts the machine – the man's dead – just then, the congressional one, he pulls out a luger he says a kraut give to him during the war which is a goddamn lie, & begins to shoot up the barbecue beef signs . . . the radio plays the star spangled banner – next day, a young arsonist, with a turtle on his head & his hands on his hips & his backbone slipping, sees me walking the donkey on the east side – 'saw you with jenny last nite – anything happening there?' i say 'oh my God, how can you ask such a thing? dont you know there are starving kids in china?' he say 'yes, but that was last nite – today's a new day' & i say 'yeah – well that's too bad – i still aint gonna tell you nothing about jenny' he calls me an idiot & i say 'here take my donkey if it'll make you feel any better – i'm on my way to the movies anyway' it is five minutes to rush hour – a strange transaction of goods takes place on third avenue – the supermarket explodes from malnutrition – God bless malnutrition

> i dont care what bob hope says – he
> aint going with you nowhere – also, john
> wayne mightve kicked cancer, but you
> oughta see his foot – forget about those
> hollywood people telling you what to do –
> theyre all gonna get killed by the indians –
> see you in your dreams
>   lovingly,
>   plastic man

Ape on Sunday

ZING & they throw him thru the door & he lands in a truck – he gets out somewhere on the Mobile line & says 'the war's going fine – aint it paleface?' & immediately makes a friend . . . 'it's nice to have friends aint it shit-brain?' this makes a stronger tie & both of 'm together – they go beat up some male secretary who works for a jockey . . . UNTOUCHABLE – they walk thru the street of

France & poison the dogs & when they get back – both receive medals for bravery 'it's nice to have medals aint it monsterass?' they cannot be separated these two friends . . . they are invited to speak at religious & college gatherings & finally become board members of the rootbeer industry 'it's nice to have all the rootbeer you can drink aint it fishturd?' an ABSOLUTE bond that cannot be broken . . . one day one of the friends discovers that he's never been doing any of the talking . . . he inquires about it but gets no response – he murders the other friend & some young punk around town – he gets put in jail for 90 years . . . everything wouldve been overlooked but John Huston – & i do mean John Huston – he made a Bible movie out of it & changed all the names – also there was nothing in the plot of course about the rootbeer stand – other'n that – it was a full drag 'i was expecting to see a bit of Mobile' – said Princess 'i was really expecting to see a bit of Mobile' – Princess is an ape – she usually goes to movies on Sunday

look you asshole – tho i might be nothing but
a butter sculptor, i refuse to go on working
with the idea of your praising as my reward –
like what are your credentials anyway? excpt for
talking about all us butter sculptors, what else
do you do? do you know what it feels like to
make some butter sculpture? do you know what
it feels like to actually ooze that butter around
& create something of fantastic worth? you said
that my last year's work 'The King's Odor' was
great & then you say i havent done anything as
great since – just who the hell are you talking to

anyway? you must have something to do in your
real life – i understand that you praised the piece
you saw yesterday entitled 'The Monkey Taster'
about which you said meant 'a nice work of butter
carved into the shape of a young man who likes
only african women' you are an idiot – it doesnt
mean that at all . . . i hereby want nothing to do
with your hangups – i really dont care what you think
of my work as i now know you dont understand it
anyway . . . i must go now – i have this new hunk of
margarine waiting in the bathtub – yes i said
MARGARINE & next week i just might decide to
use cream cheese – & i really dont care what you
think of my experimenting – you take yourself
too seriously – youre going to get an ulcer &
go into the hospital – they'll put you in a
ward where you cant have any visitors – you'll
go right off your nut – i really dont care anymore –
i am so bored with your rules & regulations
that i might not even talk to you again – just
remember tho, when you evaluate a piece of
butter, you are talking about yourself, so
you'd just better sign your name . . . see you,
if youre lucky, at mrs. keeler's cake festival

yours

Snowplow Floater

p.s. youre my friend & i'm trying to help you

collision

boss aint it awful the way
they make you look at things
as if you were inside of a toilet –

their toilet!
these sadistic nurses – they speak
to me as if i was a finger –
i lay in this bed unprotected &
the fellow next door – he must
be a Zulu – the doctors cant
stand him
& he gets no visitors – the
Sister says he's irreligious but
i just think he gags alot
boss three bodies got shipped out
this morning – Lady Esther said that
they went to the hunting ground –
Cronie said that they never were
worth much anyway & St. Crockasheet
said abracadabra – Lady Esther is
the cleaning lady & she was
mopping up the beds when i woke
up . . . there was some candle wax
on the window – Cronie said not
to touch it

there is a sign in the hall that reads 'Quiet' –
it waits for no one – i think that is
what makes people different than
signs

i say to him 'they'll get you'
& he say 'no' & i say '& if they
dont get you, you'll get yourself'
& he say 'you got bad manners &
i go to church & nobody's gonna
get me' & then some guys wearing

parachutes come in & give him
a wiff of mint & hand him a
peacock feather & then they slit
his throat . . . i looked out the
window & saw this car stop – it
had a bumper sticker saying
'Vote, Goat' & a man got out &
wiped his feet on a doormat –
he carried a book of Aesop's Fables
& then Lady Esther came in again
& cleaned up the mess – i turned
on the radio but all that was
happening was the news

boss aint it fierce the way that one
woman with the Persian monkey treated
the other woman with the Alley monkey?
Claudette came to see me last nite –
she doesnt own a monkey & she couldnt
get it – then at the same time, the nurse
came in & said 'it's raining cats &
dogs outside – is it too much for you
to bear ha ha?' i couldve swallowed her

tonite i dance with Strawberry, the
bloody clothes wife – i say her head,
if necessary, would crack like an egg
& she damns me – if i thank her
then she calls me a whore so there's
no way out . . . my mind is with the kitchen
workers but when they catch spiders &
pull their legs off & laugh – it usually
wakes me up . . . i am sick of people

praising Einstein – bourgeois ghosts –
i am sick of heroic sorrow

as soon as i get out of here
i'm going to my blood bank
& make a withdrawal & go
to Greece – Greece is beautiful
& nobody understands you
there

the janitor with a glass eye –
he's all right – at least he
minds his own business – he
tells me that Shakespeare's relatives
killed his ancestors – & that now
his brothers wont read Shakespeare . . .
he says that he used to ride to
church on a ox & when they sold
the church, he sold the ox . . .
the janitor, he's ok . . . Lady
Esther says that he aint never
gonna amount to much but i
never speak to Lady Esther &
what does she know about people
with glass eyes anyway?
my bosom feels like the
grave diggers have been at
it all nite . . . tomorrow
if i'm lucky, i'll have breakfast
in Heaven . . . some crazy fishhook dangles
thru my window – i might as well

get up & walk on my forehead –
i might as well lose all my tickets . . .
i wish there was something i
wanted as badly as this fishhook
wants to express itself

dear mister congressman:
it's about my house – some time
ago i made a deal with a syrup company
to advertise their product on the side
facing the street – it wasnt so bad at
first, but soon they put up another
ad on the other side – i didn't even
mind that, but then they plastered
these women all over the windows with
cans of syrup in their arms – in exchange
the company paid my phone & gas bill &
bought a few clothes for the tots – i told
the town council that i'd do most anything
just to let some sun in the house but they
said we couldnt offend the syrup company
because it's called Granma Washington's
Syrup & people tend to associate it with
the constitution . . . the neighbors dont help
me at all because they feel that if anything
comes off my house, it'll have to go on theirs
& none of them want their houses looking like
mine – the company offered to buy my house as a
permanent billboard sign, but God, i got my
roots here & i had to refuse at first – now they
tell me some negroes are moving in down the
block – as you can see, things dont look

too good at the moment – my eldest son is
in the army so he cant do a thing – i
would appreciate any helpful suggestion –
thank you

yours in allegiance
Zorba the Bomb

Cowboy Angel Blues

meanwhile back in texas – beautiful texas – Freud paces back
& forth – struggling with his boot & trying to finish his
Vermouth – 'fraid you got the wrong idea Mr. Clap – if i
was you, i'd give in & go chop those trees down for my
mother – after all, there's a little mother in all of us' 'yes but
i mean why do you think i do it? why do you think i inten-
tionally set fire to my bed everytime she asks me to cut
down those trees? why?' 'yes – well – Mr. Clap – perhaps
it is the womb calling – you know – perhaps when you were
a little boy, you heard a tree falling & the sound of it went
WOOOOM & now as you are older – everytime you hear
that sound – in one form or another of course – you just
want to – oh shall we say – light it up?' 'yes that seems
logical – thank you very much – i feel to go chop those trees
down now' 'ah but remember son – a tree falling in the forest
without any sound has nobody to hear it!' 'yes – well – i

shall be there then – i shall not burn my bed anymore' 'good
– let me know of your progress & if anything drastic comes
up – here – take these pills – by the way, you should call
your mother "Stella" just to show her that you mean busi-
ness – oh & while youre at it, could you chop me some
firewood please?' 'yes – all right – thank you very much
again – excuse me sir – are you having some trouble with
your boot?' 'no – no – my leg's just getting a little hairier
– that's all' . . . get back to this beautiful texas & dont swap
that cow – Corpus Christi aflame – common thieves –
maggots & millionaires trading sons & dollars & rolling
back chumps – the black gypsy lady & Buddy Holly himself
into the tanks & voids held up to Scrawny Horizon by Lee
Marvin & the forty thieves BRILLIANT & Sancho Panza
Remembered like in an Arabic moonbook & Malcolm X
Forgotten like a caught fish & wonder – ah wonder just
what – just what That means . . . Lovetown so pathetic &
the grownmen crying – the winds are anchored here & you
do not disturb these tears nor rivers – you do not take baths
in the abandoned bathtubs but rather mix electric herbs &
be watchdog to the Great White Mountain . . . Funky
Phaedra – in the center of a No Disturb sign & Black Ace
singing – she tries to outstare a bowl of money – she – as
they say – has one foot in the grave – the apprentice clown,
Tomboy, at her feet – he's known professionally as Rabbit
Rough & plays a homemade steel guitar – when loaded, he
really bites into it – Weep the Greed is watching the
happening from a caved-in mare & he lights a cigarette with
one of his stolen wanted posters . . . 'love is magic' says
Phaedra – Funky Phaedra – Rabbit dont say nothing – Weep
the Greed says 'go to it gal!' 'love is wonderful' says Phaedra
'get 'm, stranger!' says Weep the Greed – Phaedra takes off
her stetson – five bunnies & a nickel shot full of holes jump

out 'which way's laos?' says one of the bunnies 'some trick!'
says Weep the Greed – 'love is that gliding feeling' 'yipee!
& i'll be a coonbong!' says Weep the Greed 'love is gentle-
ness – softness – creaminess' says Phaedra – who is now
having a pillow fight – her weapon, a mattress – she stands
on a deserted marshmallow – her foe, some Unitarian who's
fallen off one a them high sierras & lived to tell about it –
he holds a fascist pint of yogurt 'love is riding a striped mare
across the orgy plains on barbarian sunday' screams Rabbit
Rough, the apprentice clown – this is the first thing he's said
all day & now he hesitates – Phaedra – meanwhile – is getting
beaten in the fight – 'sure it is' says Weep the Greed '& then
your mare ends up like this one – then you put your arm
in a sling – your feet in a vault & then you get a job working
for a camel – right?' Phaedra – totally wiped out from the
fight – she comes crawling back – seizes Rabbit – pulls his
shirt off – twists his arm behind his back & throws him into
the windmill – Weep the Greed gets busted by the Padres
& all the wanted posters fly over the united states – the mare
gets confiscated & held without bail . . . Mr. Clap – mean-
time – makes another visit to Freud 'only rich people can
afford you' he says 'only rich people can afford all art – isnt
that the way it is?' 'isnt that the way it always has been?'
says Freud 'ah yes' says Mr. Clap with a sigh – 'by the way
– how's the mother?' 'oh she's ok – you know her name's
Art – she makes a lot of money' 'oh?' 'yes – i've told her
all about you – you must come to the house some time' 'yes'
says Freud with a martha raye type grin 'yes – perhaps i
will' . . . Phaedra pounding her knuckles into a piece of water
– scratching her snake bites – a getaway car goes by consisting
of: three lying hunters off the Brazos River – two window-
peeking mothers each holding some decayed pictures of lili
st. cyr – a side order of bacon – some underprivileged bonus

babies shot full of dexedrine – a painter with a plate on his face – one barbell – Dracula smoking a cigarette & eating an angel – the ghost of cheetah, madame nhu & bridey murphy all wrapped in toothpaste – a box of magic wands & one innocent bystander . . . needless to say – there is no more room in the car – Phaedra scowls & she bellows 'love is going PLUMB INSANE' & wine bottle breaking – texas exploding & dinner by the sea – ship commanders with perfect features – theyre seen – theyre seen by truckdrivers – the truckdrivers complain of hijacking & see these ship commanders riding stallions into the howling Gulf of Mexico & here comes Phaedra 'love is going plumb insane' . . . she is walking by Mr. Clap – who is smiling – he wears his cap inside out – he's eating good fruit – HE'LL be all right – Mr. Clap – he'll be all right

dear buzz:
i want the bibles marked up thirty percent –
to justify the markup, i want free hairbrushes
given away with each bible – also, the chocolate
jesuses should not be sold in the south . . . one
more thing, concerning the end of the world
game – perhaps if you had some germ warfare for
it you could sell it for twice as much – things
kinda stormy round here – office in turmoil –
secretary wiped out recently – guess what happened
to the pictures of the pres? yeah well some
joker drew a earring on him in the original print
& somehow it slipped by the production staff –
needless to say, we couldn't get rid of any
of them around here that's for sure, so we had

to ship them all to puerto rico – thing worked
out ok tho – distributors down there said they
went like hot cakes . . . almost as fast as the
red white & blue hamburger sets – oh – i meant to
tell you, i think if you made the 'i voted for
the winner' buttons triangle shaped, they might
go a little faster . . . by the way, i did tell you
to send the 'i'm a beatles eater' handkerchiefs to
the dominican republic & Not to england – fraid you
made a little mistake there, buzzy boy! like i
said, office in turmoil – got a new kid but he fell
in the water cooler right away . . . he's suing us for
teeth damage – lotza problems

> see you in the cafeteria
> bosom buddy,
> syd dangerous

Subterranean Homesick Blues
& the Blond Waltz

let me say this about Justine – she was 5ft.2 & had Hungarian
eyes – her belief was that if she could make it with Bo
Diddley – she could get herself straight – now Ruthy – she
was different – she always wanted to see a cock fight – went

to Mexico City when she was 17 & a runaway castoff – she met Zonk when she was 18 – Zonk came from her home town – at least that's what he said when he met her – when they busted up, he said he never heard of the place but that's beside the point – anyway these three – they make up the Realm Crew . . . i met them exactly at their table & they took 2 years of sanction from me but i never talk much about it myself – Justine was always trying to prove she existed as if she really needed proof – Ruthy – she was always trying to prove that Bo Diddley existed & Zonk he was trying to prove that he existed just for Ruthy but later on said that he was just trying to prove he existed to himself – me? i started wondering about whether anybody existed but i never pushed it too much – especially when Zonk was around – Zonk hated himself & when he got too high he thought everybody was a mirror

one day i discovered that my secrets were punny – i tried to build them up but Justine said 'this is the Twentieth Century baby – i mean you know – like they dont do that anymore – when dont you go walk on the street – that'll build up your secrets – it's no use to spend all these hours a day doing it in a room – youre losing living – i mean like if you wanna be some kinda charles atlas, go right ahead . . . but you better head off for muscle beach – i mean you just might as well snatch jayne mansfield – become king of your kind & start some kind of secret gymnasium' . . . after being ridiculed to such a degree – i decided to leave my secrets alone & Justine – Justine was right – my secrets got bigger – in fact they grew so big that they outweighed my body . . . i hitchhiked alot in those days & you had to be ready – you never knew what kind of people you were gonna meet on the road i sang in a forest one day & someone said it was three o'clock – that nite when i read the newspaper, i saw that a tenement had been set aflame & that three firemen & nineteen people had lost their lives – the fire was at three o'clock too . . . that nite in a dream i was singing again – i was singing the same song in the same forest & at the same time – in the dream there was also a tenement blazing . . . there was no fog & the dream was clear – it was not worth analyzing as nothing is worth analyzing – you learn from a conglomeration of the incredible past – whatever experience gotten in any way whatsoever – controlling at once the present tense of the problem – more or less like a roy rogers & trigger relationship of which under present western standards is an impossibility – me singing – i moved from the forest – frozen in a moment & picked up & moved above land – the tenement blazing too at the same moment being picked up & moved towards me – i, still singing & this building still buring . . . needless to say – i & the building met & as instantly as it stopped, the motion started again – me, singing & the building burning – there i was – in all truth – singing in front of a raging fire – i was unable to do anything about this fire – you see – not because i was lazy or loved to watch good fires – but rather because both myself & the fire were in the same Time all right but we were not in the same Space – the only thing we had in common was that we existed in the same moment . . . i could not feel any guilt about just standing there singing for as i said i was picked up & moved there not by my own free will but rather by some unbelievable force – i told Justine about this dream & she said 'that's right – lot of people would feel guilty & close their eyes to such a happening – these are people that interrupt & interfere in other people's lives – only God can be everywhere at the same Time & Space – you are human – sad & silly as it might seem' . . . i got very drunk that afternoon & a mysterious confusion entered into my body – 'when i hear of the bombings, i see red & mad hatred' said Zonk – 'when i hear of the bombings, i see the head of a dead nun' said i – Zonk said 'what?' . . . i have never taken my singing – let alone my other habits – very seriously – ever since then – i have just accepted it – exactly as i would any other crime

the soldier with the long beard says go ask questions my son but the shaggy orphan says that it's all a hype – the bearded soldier says what's a hype? & the shaggy orphan says what's a son? the taste of bread is common yet who can & who cares to tell someone else what it tastes like – it tastes like bread that's what it tastes like . . . to find out why Bertha shouldnt push the man off the flying trapeze you dont find out by thinking about it – you find out by being Bertha – that's how you find out

let me say this about Justine – Ruthy & Zonk – none of them understood each other at all – Justine – she went off to join a rock n roll band & Ruthy – she decided to fight cocks professionally & when last heard from, Zonk was working in the garment district . . . they all lived happily ever after

where i live now, the only thing that keeps
the area going is tradition – as you can figure
out – it doesnt count very much – everything
around me rots . . . i dont know how long it has
been this way, but if it keeps up, soon
i will be an old man – & i am only 15 – the only
job around here is mining – but jesus, who wants

to be a miner . . . i refuse to be part of such
a shallow death – everybody talks about the middle
ages as if it was actually in the middle ages –
i'll do anything to leave here – my mind
is running down the river – i'd sell my
soul to the elephant – i'd cheat the sphinx –
i'd lie to the conqueror . . . tho you might
not take this the right way, i would even
sign a chain with the devil . . . please dont
send me anymore grandfather clocks – no more
books or care packages . . . if you're going to
send me something, send me a key – i shall
find the door to where it fits, if it takes
me the rest of my life

                                    your friend
                                    Friend

Furious Simon's Nasty Humor

i had a dream
that the cook
leaned
& shook
his fist over the
balcony & said yes

to the people
yes the people
& he said this
to the people
'i want four cups of stormtrooper –
a tablespoon of catholic – five hideous paranoids –
some water buffalo – a half pound of communist –
six cups of rebel – two cute atheists –
a quart bottle of rabbi – one teaspoon of
bitter liberal – some antibirth tablets –
three fourths black nationalist –
a dab of lemon cock powder –
some mogen david capitalists & a whole lot
of fat people with extra money'
then the cook's helper
appeared
& cleared his throat & then he
said to the people yes the
people
'also we'd like a mocking bird
& some maids in milking – some raped
college students & a drenched hen –
two turtle gloves
& a partridge & a gin & a pear tree'
i awoke from this dream
in the state of fright – then jumped out of bed &
ran for the kitchen – crashed thru the door &
slammed on the light/ fell on my
bended knees &
thanked God
that there was nothing new in
the ice box

dear Puck,
traded in my electric guitar for
one you call a gut one . . . you can play
it all by yourself – dont need a band –
eliminates all the fighting except of
course for the other gut guitar
players – am doing well – have no idea of
what's happening but all these girls
with moustaches, theyre going crazy
over me – you must try them sometime –
weather is good – threw away all my lefty
frizzell records – also got rid of my
parka – you can keep my cow as i now am
on the road to freedom

see yuh later aligator
Franky Duck

I Found the Piano Player Very Crosseyed But Extremely Solid

he came with his wrists taped & he carried his own coat
hanger – i could tell at a glance that he had no need for
Sonny Rollins but i asked him anyway 'whatever happened
to gregory corso?' he just stood there – he took out a deck

of cards & he replied 'wanna play some cards?' to which
i answered 'no but whatever happened to jane russell?' he
flapped the cards & they went sailing all over the room
'my father taught me that' he said 'it's called 52 pickup but
i call it 49 pickup cause i'm shy three cards – haw haw aint
that a scream & which one's the piano?' at this gesture i
was relieved to see that he was human – not a saint mind
you – & he wasn't very likable – but nevertheless – he was
human – 'that's my piano over there' i say 'the one with
the teeth' he immediately rambled over & he stomped hard
across the floor 'shhhhhh' i said 'you'll wake up my No
Pets Allowed sign' he shrugged his shoulders & took out
a piece of chalk – he began to draw a picture of his kid on
my piano 'hey now look – that aint what's wrong with my
piano – i mean now dont take it personally – it's got nothing
to do with you, but my piano is out of tune – now i don't
care how you go about it but fix it – fix it right' 'my kid's
gonna be an astronaut' 'i should hope so' says me '& by
the way – could you tell me what happened to julius larosa?'
a picture of abraham lincoln falls from the ceiling 'that guy
looks like a girl – i saw him on Shindig – he's a fag' 'how
wise you are' says i 'hurry & fix my piano willya – i have
this geisha girl coming over at midnight & she digs to jump
on it' 'my kid's gonna be an astronaut' 'c'mon – get to
work – my piano – my piano – c'mon it's out of tune' at
this time, he takes out his tool & starts to tinkle on a few
high notes – 'yeah it's out of tune' he says 'but it's also
5:30' 'so what?' i say most melancholy 'so it's quitting time
– that's so what' 'quitting time?' 'look buddy i'm a union
man . . .' 'look yourself – you ever heard of woody guthrie?
he was a union man too & he fought to organize unions
like yers & he dug people's needs & do you know what
he'd say if he knew that a union man – an honest-to-God

union man – was walking out on a poor hard traveling cat's needs – do you know what he'd say d'yuh know what he'd think?' 'all right i'm getting sick of you sprouting out names at me – i never hearda no boody guppie & anyway . . .' 'woody guthrie not boody guppie!' 'yeah well anyway i don't know what he'd say, but tomorrow – now if you want a new man tomorrow – like you can just call up & the union'll send you over one gladly – like i dont care – it's just another job to me buddy – just another job to me' 'WHAT! you dont even take any pride in your work? i can't believe this! do you know what boody guppie would do to you man? i mean do you know what he'd think of you?' 'i'm going home – i hate it here – it's just not my style at all & anyway i never heard of any coody puppie' 'boody guppie, you miserable bosom – not coody puppie & get out of my house – get out this instant!' 'my kid's gonna be an astronaut' 'i don't care – you cant bribe me – i'm bigger'n that – get out – get out' . . . after he leaves i try playing my piano – no use – it sounds like a bowling alley – i change my No Pets Allowed sign to a Home Sweet Home sign & wonder why i havent any friends . . . it starts to rain – the rain sounds like a pencil sharpener – i look out the window & everybody's walking around without a hat – it is 5:31 – time to celebrate someone's birthday – the piano tuner has left his coat hanger behind . . . which really brings me down

unfortunately my friend, you shall not get
the information you seek out of me – i, my
good man, am not a fink! none of my relatives
are or have been related to benedict arnold
& i myself despise john wilkes booth – i dont

smoke marijuana & my family hates italian
food – none of my friends like black & white
movies & again myself, i have never seen a
russian ballet – also, i have started an organization
to turn in all people that laugh at
newsreels – so: could you please stop those
letters to the district attorney saying that
i know who murdered my wife – my principles are
at stake here – i would NOT sacrifice them for
one moment of pleasure – i am an honest man

yours in growth,
ivan the bloodburst

The Vandals Took the Handles
(An Opera)

to South Duchess County comes Them & Woolworth's
Fool & triumphant alice toklas, the National Bank in short
sleeves & the regulars – the sincereful regulars – House on
its final kick – still breeding & a cellarful of imaginary
Russian peasant girls holding triangles – the triangles are
real – House on Doomstown, an academy – a priest with
his winnings from Reno coming in on a parachute . . . 'inte-
grate the house!' 'only if you wish to live where youre not

wanted' 'then bomb the house!' 'only if you wish to live there by yourself' 'what do you suggest then?' 'it's a pointless house – leave it alone – it is not happy within itself – it breeds disaster – it forces you to learn things that have nothing to do with the outside world & then it kicks you out there – the house dont need you – why should you be so low as to need it – leave – go far away from the house' 'no, my friend, your way of thinking is called giving up' 'do as you wish, your way is called losing – it's not even a way of thinking' the priest leaves with his eyes downward – he is examining the rocks but he's forgotten that his parachute has already been used once . . . alice toklas lays on a grassy knoll & blesses a flower 'oh the enemy – beware of the enemy – the enemy is santa claus!' . . . the flower doesnt need her – the flower needs rain

we sat in a room where Harold, who called himself 'Lord of dead animals,' was climbing down from a ladder & he said 'friend or doe? friend or doe?' he wore a black shawl & someone said that he experimented in the depth of mirrors – Poncho was very startled & screamed 'i'll give you a friend or doe, you freak!' & banged him with a judo chop & stuck his head thru the ladder – 'shouldnt done that' said a very manly girl who came down the chimney 'he's very sullen but he's a good cat – does anybody want a piece of bread?' Poncho said that he wanted a piece of kidney – i said i wanted a piece of separate . . . the girl began to cry

in the photographs – you see the sand at Nice & Tangier & all the medicine men looking elegant & then out come the radar slaves – each one wanting to be an apostle & they carry the electrograms – we call them Employment & each one says things like 'haul away ho' & 'heave 'm johnny' & 'I dont dig harry james at all!' & Hefty Bore, a leftover horror from the beat generation & a dubious health freak saying to his bewildered birdgirl, WeeWee the Dyke, 'oh c'mon – it wouldnt cost you nothing to tell everybody that i'm the hippest person you ever met – c'mon – i do lots of things for you!' & Wee Wee saying 'but i never see anybody – you never let me see anybody!' & then Olive, who once started a streetfight over Carl Perkins' eyes & now builds laugh machines for rich democrats – he brings in the equipment & you get taken across a narrow bridge where hundreds of tourists follow & sail lead weight records at your feet & they place you in a giant bus horn & voices yelling 'i want that one – i want that one!' Madame Remember appears & she takes away your photographs & all that's left in the outside world is your hand – little babies bite it & mothers are screaming SCREAMING 'yes – he can have my vote – i'll vote for him any day' . . . now youre a plastic vein – youve vanished inside of a perfect message – historic phone calls come thru to your belly & curious tabernacles move slowly thru your mind – hitchhiking – hitchhiking unashamed thru the goofs of your brain – your ideals are gone & all that remains are the cutup photographs of you standing in the supermarket – the bus still runs but now you take cabs with the jungle boys . . . Egotist shows you his diary & he says 'I've learned to be silent' & you say 'you've learned nothing – youve just said something'

the good folks around here, they got plenty of questions – they beat elephants to death with candy sticks – 'a white bear is a crazy bear' say the thieves who really are not thieves but rather plain people who dont expect their friends to get sick so they'll need them – there is an illness

on the mountain & a polio lily grew out of a green purse
last Sunday – a dangerous nickel lays on the town square
. . . everybody watches to see who'll pick it up . . . TO
SEARCH IS TO NEGLECT & VIOLENT LUCK IS
STAMPEDE & there's a bunch of us around here but we
only pick up dollars

here lies bob dylan
murdered
from behind
by trembling flesh
who after being refused by Lazarus,
jumped on him
for solitude
but was amazed to discover
that he was already
a streetcar &
that was exactly the end
of bob dylan

he now lies in Mrs Actually's
beauty parlor
God rest his soul
& his rudeness

two brothers
& a naked mama's boy
who looks like Jesus Christ
can now share the remains
of his sickness
& his phone numbers

there is no strength
to give away –
everybody now
can just have it back

here lies bob dylan
demolished by Vienna politeness –
which will now claim to have invented him
the cool people can
now write Fugues about him
& Cupid can now kick over his kerosene lamp –
boy dylan – killed by a discarded Oedipus
who turned
around
to investigate a ghost
& discovered that
the ghost too
was more than one person

South Duchess County importing pyramid & scavengers
by the truckload & Cousin Butch – he leaves now & then
to make three dollars a nite telling about the flying saucers
. . . a warmonger – Antonio – working day & nite in a
garage – he smuggles pad locks to the olympic swimmers
& hires out women for the baseball players – he's very
quiet & very fashion conscious – he knows his religious
geography – he's training his kid to be a gorilla & then he
will rent him out for people's closets – he says his right
hand holds war but his left hand holds a wet paranoid smile
. . . the peacemonger – Roach – when last seen – was chasing
a train – says that his right hand holds peace but his left
hand was seen holding a doorknob & a meathook . . . South

Duchess County in bandages & little Lady Suntan trying
to analyze the Albino terrorists . . . South Duchess County
– pure as visions & uneducated – shall exist past the deadly
complements to it – past its lack of holidays & past the
possible

you cant fool me – im too smart – you
were on that subway train when that
kid got knifed – you just sat there – you
were on the street when that black car
drove up & tossed some form in the
river – you turned around & walked to a
phone & pretended you had someone to call . . .
you were also there when they castrated
that poor boy in public – you cant fool me –
youre not so tough – sure, you took a big
stand on juvenile delinquency – you said to
run all the hoods out of town – oh youre so
brave – sure, you say youre patriotic – you
say youre not scared to drop any H bomb &
show everybody that you mean what you say
but you dont say anything excpt that youre
not scared to drop any H bombs – how can you
say that my kids must learn from a good
example? they can learn from a bad example
just as well – they can learn from you as well
as me – you can't have me under your thumb
anymore – not because i'm too squirmy, but because
your hands are made of water . . . when you wish
to talk to me, let me know ahead of time – i'll
have a bucket waiting . . . just because your wife
is pregnant, you've no license to meddle in mine

or my friends' affairs – ask your wife if she
remembers me

yours faithfully
Simon Dord

p.s. you probably remember me as

Julius the Honk

A Sheriff in the Machinery

Fringe – the boy lunatic – conceived on an Ash Wednesday
when Scrounge meets Suckup girl – now Scrounge, he's
twisted – he's completed wacked – ever since a midget (who
turned out be be a child actor smoking a cigar) stomped
on him like a balloon. Scrounge just aint never been the
same – it's been said that he paralyzed his home-town soda
jerk & if he didn't like you, he'd turn the jerk loose on
you – to my knowledge, this never happened . . . Suckup
girl – her nosejob keeps dripping & she has to carry a
gardener along when she goes to parties – she is talking to
Bishop Freeze, who asks her 'whaja thinka that Monet
painting? i mean i just got done spending five days reading
Kierkegaard – alone in a room baby – just me &
Kierkegaard – yeah – & the first thing i see when i come
outa there is that painting – well! flip? lemme tell you did
i flip? i mean did you dig the wisdom in that goddamn

forehead? did you dig the crumbs in the chick's smile?' 'yes
i found it extremely . . . i found it extremely . . .' 'mono-
graphic?' says Scrounge trying to help her out & put the
make on her 'yes & also i found it voluptuously interesting'
when Bishop Freeze goes home, Suckup comes over to
Scrounge & thanks him 'dont mention it' says Scrounge
who unbuttons his shirt & shows her his name signed on
his stomach 'had that done in Kadalawoppa last year –
that's in Mexico you know' 'oh that's donkey country – i
know it very well – the beaches are extremely fantastic –
i hear the fuzz are down there now tho' 'yeah baby the
fuzz come in about last Christmas – the scene now is in
the jungle' 'would you like to go for a ride on my stallion
– we'll drop the gardener off' 'yeah baby sure – then maybe
we'll come back & shoot the bull' 'all right – sounds wizzy
– i got my gun & we can talk about Kadalawoppa & every-
thing' 'Kadalawoppa yeah & did you ever known Puny
Jim down there?' 'no but what about Lupe d'Lupe – did
you know him – he's a retired coffee expert – comes from
the coast?' 'yes – oh my god – yes i did – i found him
extremely uh . . . extremely . . .' 'he's a natural baby – he's
a natural – a meth-head but he's all beautiful – he's the one
that showed me that the jungle was there' 'yes me too – i
found him extremely interesting' . . . nite falls now &
Scrounge takes Suckup girl by the leg – she rearranges her
mouth & they both go out the back door looking at the
moon . . . Fringe is conceived

a greasy fat newspaper lays on Roger's counter – Roger,
the owner of Cafe de la All Nite – a spanish all nite restau-
rant – is sad for the first time in 9 months – his mother
has disappeared in Paris & he fears now that all those
frenchmen might have their fun over what they think is

her dead body . . . roger glances thru the facts of the fat greasy newspaper – a tiger stampede in hollywood – annette & frankie avalon found in pacific ocean – hands tied behind their backs – footage of bugs bunny documentary found in the lungs of tom mix, whom everybody thought was dead but showed up as a boxtop – rebels attack Walgreen's in Fantasia – dictator wires for more candy – U.S. sending in marines & arnold stang – in Phoenix, man eats his wife at 2 in the afternoon – FBI investigating/ bomb explodes in norman mailer's pantry – leaves him color blind – big shakeup in sports department – ed sullivan & Freshkid, a relative of Prince Rainier & visiting this country as a guest of Cong Long, a grandson of Huey Long – seen escaping with catchers' mitts – contact lenses & dope tablets – Bishop Sheen very disturbed – when asked for opinion – just stated 'i cant believe it – i cant believe this could happen to ed – it mustve been the company he's been keeping lately' – william buckshot junior writing oriental cookbook – is very upset that he's lived after falling off diving board with no water in pool – walter crankcase arrested in Utah for lifting candles – when questioned, he calmly explained that he needed them to listen to some early little richard records – Doctor Sponge, inventor of deer poison & snap crackle & pop cereal – willing to take case for slight fee/ little girls spray chancellor erhard with goose fat on his arrival from miami – president lets embarrassing fart at banquet table – blames it on the eggs – stock market takes worst dive in years – in gary, indiana, colored man shot twenty times thru the head – coroner says cause of death is unknown . . . no good movies playing in town & only one job in the want ads – NEEDED: a honest man to be rag picker for friendly family – must be sturdy – preferably a basketball player – must have a love for children – couch & a toilet – wages to be discussed – phone TOongee 1965 . . . Roger puts down his greasy paper & who should come in but Scrounge the Suckup girl – it is early morning & they are not lovers anymore – they are customers

9 months later, Fringe is born – he wears short pants – goes to college – gets a job for a war magazine – he marries a nice plump girl whose father is a natural winner/ Fringe meets more & more people – he goes on a diet & then he dies

to my students:
i take it for granted that youve all read
& understand freud – dostoevsky – st.
michael – confucius – coco joe – einstein –
melville – porgy snaker – john zulu – kafka –
sartre – smallfry – & tolstoy – all right then –
what my work is – is merely picking up where
they left off – nothing more – there you have
it in a nutshell – now i'm giving you my
book – i expect you all to jump right in –
the exam will be in two weeks – everybody
has to bring their own eraser.

your professor
herold the professor

False Eyelash in Maria's Transmission

maria – she's mexican – but she's american as Howling Wolf – 'my worried mind, it annoys me! i cant take my rest! i'm disgusting!' says her brother, who sneaks across the border & gets drunk on skinny whores & Turkish gas – 'maria needs a shot' says King Villager 'she needs a shot of a very bored God' – the rest of the villagers sing a song that sounds like 'oh the days of forty-nine' in a Welsh accent & Adlai Stevenson starting a riot on the mountaintop . . . maria once nailed coffins for a living – 'i will bust a plateglass window over Adlai Stevenson's head!' says her brother very drunk on Turkish gas 'i will prove to him that he too is a masochist – i shall make him bend like a woman & wish he was on a freight train to Frisco' – a marine with his finger nibbled – Josephine – whose grandfather died at Shiloh – stabbed maria once & hid her clothes – she was arrested on an incest charge . . . King Villager, who is slowly dying of cancer, polishes his noisy beard now & mutters 'cops – progress – american monuments' & 'nothing matters' maria has made love with a beggar recently – he was disguised in flamboyant tinfoil – they made it in a saddlebag – she can run a mile in 5 days point 9 & the traveling roadshow that comes thru the town once a year respects her for it . . . maria's father lays dead on the hill – rich pimps – humanity & civilization walk over his grave to show her that they mean business . . . she is not going on any goodwill tours this year – there is a false eyelash in her transmission . . . there is not many places she can taste

this is my last letter – i've tried to
please you, but i see now that you have
too much on your mind – what you need is
someone to flatter you – i would do that, but
what would be the worth? after all, i
need nothing from you – you are so much
tied up in, though, that you have turned
into a piece of hunger – while the mystics
of the world jump in the sun, you have
turned into a lampshade – if youre going to think,
dont think about why people dont love each
other – think about why they dont love themselves –
maybe then, you will begin to love them – if
you have something to say, let me know, i'm
just around the corner, located by the flight
controls – take it easy & dont scratch too
much – watch the green peppers & i think youve
had enough popcorn – youre turning into an addict –
as i said, there's simply nothing i can give
you excpt a simply – there is nothing i can take
from you excpt a guilty conscience – i cant give
nor take any habit . . . see you at the masquerade
ball

tormentedly
water boy

Al Aaraaf & the Forcing Committee

now the anarchist – we call him Moan – he takes us & Medusa
– she carries the wigs – Moan carries the maps – by noon,
we're in Abyss Hallway – there are shadows of jugglers on
the wall & from out of the Chelsea part of the ceiling drops
Monk – Moan's boy – Medusa going into a room with two
swords above the door – some removable mirrors inside –
Medusa disappears . . . Lacky, a strange counterpart of the
organization – he comes out of the room carrying a mirror
– both swords above the door fall down – one sticks into the
floor – the other slices him in half . . . Monk, typical flunky
& writer of eccentric gag lines to tell yourself if youre ever
hung up in the Andes – he leads us into a room with Chinese
sayings that all read 'a penny slaved is a penny is a penny is
a penny' . . . there is a gigantic looking glass & Monk imme-
diately disintegrates . . . after lunch, you hear a punch of
rocks & car accidents over a loudspeaker & Chang Chung –
some transient & a professional extra sensual bum without
any pride or shame & he's selling rebel war cries & 'how to
become a birth control pill' pamphlets – 'invent me a signa-
ture' says Moan 'i must go sign some papers concerning the
zippers of truth' 'zippers of truth!' says Chang Chung 'there
is no truth!' 'right' says Moan 'but there are zippers' 'very
sorry – velly solly – it is my mistake – it's just that i'm wearing
huge shoes today that's all 'dont let it happen again' says
Moan staring down to his own shoes . . . down the hallway
now in a wheelchair comes Photochick – she is the flower
of Moan & she's eating a cowpie

Grady O'lady comes in – gives everybody the nod & wants to know where she can get a maid – 'dig henry miller?' she asks kind of snaky like – 'you mean that fantastically dead henry miller? the real estate agent henry miller?' 'what you mean?' say Grady O'lady 'henry's not a real estate agent – he's a cavedweller – he's an artist – he writes about God' 'i'm thinking of another henry miller – i'm thinking of the one that wears a tulip in his crotch & writes about cecil b. de mille's girls . . . O'lady takes an orange out of her pocket 'got this in the Aztec country – watch me now boys' she takes the orange & squeezes it very gently & slowly – then she rips it open madly & snarls & it oozes & dribbles down her mouth – all over her shirt – more – more – she's all covered in orange – Moan comes in with his art critic – Sean Checkshit & both of them – they start discussing a shipping deal 'Junior Bork has just finished his novel on World War I – speaks very good for our side & we must remember not to use it for toilet paper' 'i'm going to use it for toilet paper' says Photochick 'explain yourself!' says Moan & Photochick explains that one person's truth is always someone else's lie & Moan he starts whipping her with his map & she starts crying & walks into a room with mirrors & blows up – 'now back to this shipping deal' says Moan, who turns around to find Sean Checkshit on the floor with Grady O'lady & theyre both covered in orange 'tell me more about this henry miller' says Sean 'oo ah isnt it wonderful' says Grady O'lady

in Ponce de Leon land – the union leader – Stormy Leader – is on exhibition fighting a lady wrestler . . . out of his past appears Insanely Hoppy screaming & dancing Screaming – pouting 'the world belongs to the woikas – the woikas – none of you want to be woikas – none of you – none of you could make it – none of you' 'shut up!' says Moan, who comes in the room unnoticed 'shut up – i've got a backache & anyway it's workers not woikas!' 'the world is his – it's his that looks like a walrus & moves about like a walrus & has to sleep with a wife that feels like a walrus & he's forced to be a walrus for a buncha nagging kids & he goes to nagging walrus ball games & plays poker with a bunch of walruses & then he's driven into the earth & buried with a walrus in his mouth – i dare not say enough about him – he lives in his armpit & he hates you – he has no need for you – you clutter his life – you are lucky to be hanging around in his world – you have no choice excpt to walk naked – why be so honorable about it – why be so honorable about sleeping with pigs?' CRASH 'put that boy in with proverb writers – but give him a bad review & say that he beat his wife & ate pork – say that he ate meat on Friday – say anything – just get him out of here till he's ready for training' . . . a lost pony express rider peers out from the trap door – he is carrying a picture of a long corridor & he sort of blows out his words when he talks 'you are all fools! you cant add! you can count to a million but none of you – none of you – can see the sum total of the ground on which you stand on' Darling the Hypocrite immediately lights a fire to the floor & People Gringo pounds his fist on a book & says that rocking chair & water-melon are the same word only with different letters . . . St. Bread from the riot squad – entering with his chess pieces & a hilarious hard on & he laughs too

    mother say go in That direction & please
    do the greatest deed of all time & say i say
    mother but it's already been done & she say

well what else is there for you to do & i say
i dont know mother, but i'm not going in That
direction – i'm going in that direction & she
say ok but where will you be & i say i dont
know mother but i'm not tom joad & she say
all right then i am not your mother

prince hamlet of his hexagram – sheik of unsanitary angels
– he rides on a bareback instrument – exact factor concerning
the reality of grandstand – Taj Mahal & Clytia's sundial
missing – this exact factor missing . . . nevertheless – the
bubbling under does not disturb him – Lilith teaches her
new husband, Bubba, how to use deodorant – also she
teaches him that 'stinky doo doo' means nasty filth & both
of these teachings together add up to Bubbling Under
Number One . . . Obie Doesnt – whose eyes are waxed &
that they say lives in a world of his own – he keeps repeating
'these aint normal people are they? are they? oh my God –
pass the crackers – these arent normal people are they? hello
hello can you hear me?' 'yes yes it's true – they are – they
are the normal people' says prince – who gives Obie a little
tickle – makes him laugh 'but remember – it's like the boogie
man told the centaur when the centaur invaded the territory
of the Giant Mother Geese, 'you dont have to be around
those people' – by the way, i've heard you live in a world
of your own' 'yes it's true' says Obie '& i also don't go to
birthday parties' 'very good' says the prince 'keep up the
good work' . . . about this bareback instrument – some-
times the prince is sure he's on it but not so sure he's riding
on it – at other times, he's sure he's riding on it, but not so
sure it's bareback – at odd moments, the prince is sure that
he's riding on something bareback but not so sure it's an

instrument . . . all his daily adventures, unsuccessful potatoes & other pirates try to pin him down to Certainality & put him in his place once & for all 'care to arm wrestle?' say some – 'youre a phony – youre no prince!' say the smarter ones who go into bathtubs & ask for the usual . . . the prince sees many jacks & jills come tumbling down 'funny how when you look, you cant find any pieces to pick up' he says this usually once a day to his bareback instrument – who never talks back – most good souls dont

it is not that is no Receptive for anything written or acted in the first person – it is just that there is no Second person

MAMMOTH NOAH & the oriental marauders all on the morality rap & Priest of Harmony in a narrow costume – he's with the angels now & he says 'all's useless – useless' & Instinct, poet of the antique zenith – putting on his hoofs & whinnying 'all's not useless – all is very signifying!' & the insane piper stealing the Queen's Pawn & the conquering war cry 'neither – neither' & jails being cremated & jails falling & newly arrived spirits digging – digging their fingernails – their fingernails into each other . . . Goal-Hari Cari & the Cruel Mother teasing at your harmless fate . . . the sight of george raft – richard nixon – liberace – d.h. lawrence & pablo casals – all the same person – & struggle – struggle & your weapons of curls blowing & Digging – Digging Everything

aretha – known in gallup as number 69 – in wheeling as the cat's in heat – in pittsburgh as number 5 – in brownsville as the left road, the lonesome sound – in atlanta as

dont dance, listen – in bowling green as
oh no, no not again – she's known as horse
chick up in cheyenne – in new york she's
known as just plain aretha . . . i shall play
her as my trump card

i would like to do something worthwhile like perhaps plant
a tree on the ocean but i am just a guitar player – with no
absurd fears of her reputation, Black Gal co-exists with
melody & i want to feel my evaporation like Black Gal feels
her co-existence . . . i do not want to carry a pitchfork

prince hamlet – he's somewhere on the totem pole – he
hums a shallow little tune 'oh killing me by the grave' –
aretha – lady godiva of the migrants – she sings too . . .
there are a lot of historians under the totem pole – all
pretending to be making a living – there's also a lot of spies
& customs agents – the popes dont quit & the artists live
in the meantime – the meantime dies & in its place comes
the sometimes – there is never any real sometime & the
customs agents & spies usually turn into star ice skaters on
a winter vacation & they brood about the meantime/ they
usually dont know anybody under the totem pole excpt
their elders . . . San Francisco freezing & New York neath
spells of Poe & famous barbarians 'you can make it if you
have nothing' lips prince to a spaghetti dinner – wasting
away on a slushy rink – belonging to nobody & the lumber-
jacks are coming 'i'm searching – i'm searching for some
kind of meaning!' says Jug the Lady, an escaped werewolf
– she wears a chrome head piece & has been studying
Yugoslavia for the past ten months – she has a built-in
jukebox on her motorcycle 'your mind is small – it is limited

– what kind of sense must you need–' says prince 'i want to be on the totem pole too' she confides 'the lumberjacks are coming' says prince & then he takes out his shirt tail & begins to draw circles on the air 'there are magnets on this shirt tail & they all pick up pieces of minute – now you see – i've got something to do – why'n you go see this fellow – Moan is his name – he'll straighten you – & if he cant – he knows someone that can' one of Jug's friends, a drummer who doesnt drum but rather just drops his sticks on the drums – comes out of the bushes – rather a sadist type & whose entire wardrobe consists of a marine's uniform & a washed out nurse's outfit – he yells 'i'm looking for a partner – gimme some secrets!' & then there's two little boys playing & one says 'if i owned the world, each man would have a million dollars' & one says 'if i owned the world – each man would have the chance to save the world once in his lifetime' . . . prince hamlet of his hexagram – he pulls a train & makes love to miss Julie Ann Johnson 'i said gimme some secrets – i'm just the usual beer' says this drummer & prince carves Memphis – London & Viet Nam into the pole 'there are only a few things that exist: Boogie Woogie – highpowered frogs – Nashville Blues – harmonicas walking – 80 moons & sleeping midgets – there are only three things that continue: Life – Death & the lumberjacks are coming'